TELL ME EVERY THING

Sarah Enni

Scholastic Press / New York

Library of Congress Cataloging-in-Publication Data available

ISBN 978-1-338-13915-0

10 9 8 7 6 5 4 3 2 1   19 20 21 22 23

Printed in the U.S.A.   23
First edition, March 2019
Book design by Nina Goffi

To my family

CHAPTER 1

I'm starting to worry that Smarty-Pants Camp is going to ruin my best friend, Harold.

Okay, okay. I shouldn't call it "Smarty-Pants Camp." It's a National Scholar of Promise summer program at Stanford that's super hard to get into—the most recent under-eighteen world-chess champion got wait-listed. Harold got in on the first try. I'm super proud of him.

But now, before we've even had a full week of summer break, I'm worried as I watch him stuff a Mathletes duffel bag with every collared shirt he owns.

Harold owns a lot of collared shirts.

I'm trying to tell him about LingoSpatial, a company that's replacing GPS coordinates with words. According to them, Harold's bedroom is located at "Sheep, Monarchy, Bespoke," otherwise known as 12 Waves Lane, in Sudden Cove, California, in the U.S. of A.

This is exactly the kind of thing that riles Harold up. When he gets on a really good rant, his face twists up into an unhinged half smile and his eyes take on a deranged twinkle. It's the best.

I'm perched on the edge of his desk chair, eagerly awaiting a lecture about how ludicrous it is to assume language could be more universal than numbers.

Instead, Harold merely huffs his disdain, shaking his head as he folds, then refolds, a navy-blue polo shirt. I swivel the chair, spouting some of the more insane tidbits about LingoSpatial's plot for world domination. Harold just moves on to a red polo. He's got a closet full of Ralph Lauren to starch, fold, and stack.

Yuck. I officially hate camp. It's taking my best friend away for the summer, and as far as I'm concerned, it's already got him.

His room is cramped. I have to tilt my feet back and forth to make room as he walks from closet to bed, where his large wheeled suitcase is already ridiculously full. Dusk light streams through the window, reflecting a riot of sherbet colors in the room's only mirror, mounted on the newspaper wall. Every time he reads an interesting article, Harold cuts it out (or prints it and then cuts it out) and Mod Podges it to the wall. The bylines go up to my forehead, creating the effect of one giant front page. I like to examine myself in that mirror and pretend I'm news. And today, with sandy blond bangs at peak unruly, lips sourly pursed, and a bathing suit top peeking out from under a loose knit sweater, my reflection could pass as a petulant pop starlet's mug shot.

"This suuuuuuuucks." I throw my head back and spin in the chair the way Harold hates. "What happened to that other camp, the one about starting a revolution?"

"It was Civic Engagement and Leadership Camp," he says, equally grumpy. "And I got into that one, too. But you can't say no to National Scholars of Promise, or Stanford."

"You mean your parents wouldn't *let you* say no."

He shrugs. "Same difference."

"That leadership camp was just over the mountain, in San Jose. You could have made all the protest signs your heart desired!" I whine. "You could have slept in your own bed. Helped me finish the ultimate Jeff Goldblum marathon. Taught me to drive a stick shift."

"I don't want to be gone all summer, either, Ivy. But this is a big opportunity."

I know that. But Harold's life is one long string of big opportunities—the only thing higher than his grades are his aspirations. He's never found a club he didn't want to join, or a cause he wasn't ready to lead a union strike over. He likes taking a stand, and appreciates a dramatic moment. His passion, drive, and willingness to put himself out there have opened a bunch of doors. Awards committees, scholarship funds, and our local NPR station have all called him a "kid who's going places."

They're right, duh. But he better not go places too fast. We're only rising sophomores, and I really do need to learn to drive a stick shift.

"I'm gonna beat your high score on the Boardwalk's Skee-Ball machine."

That gets him. Harold gives me a look that says, *You wouldn't dare.*

"You wouldn't dare."

"Try me!" I push off the desk to whir around even faster.

"Ivy!" he warns. With a sigh, he grabs the back of the chair and holds it still. I give him an icy pout.

"C'mon, man," I say. "Be present, in this moment, at Sheep, Monarchy, Bespoke!"

"That system is ridiculous and I won't acknowledge it," Harold says, waving me off. Then he sighs. "This is hard! I'm not packing for hiking or craft hour at the mess. We're gonna be on the Stanford campus, in their actual labs . . ." He runs a hand over his freshly shorn head, the coarse black curls cut down to the scalp. If he's playing with imaginary hair, he must really be stressed.

"Okay, okay." I stand and join him in an observe-the-closet pose. "Honestly, I don't know why you're so worried. Wouldn't it be *worse* if you had to pack for hiking and crafting and s'mores-ing? Labs be your jam!"

"Yeah but is it, like, a *casual* lab environment? Will there be coats? Will the coats be bleached white, or eggshell? Should I wear sandals with socks, just to fit in?"

I grab Harold by the shoulders and shake. "Don't even joke about that!"

He starts tearing shirts off hangers and tossing them in a heap on his bed. I know Harold's already thinking about the metric

4

system, and lab reports, and jockeying to stand out among the smartest high school students in the United States.

Meanwhile, I'm noting how the dying sunlight deepens the contrast between Harold's dark brown skin and the ink-covered wall of clippings behind him. I take a mental picture, trying to capture movement in the imagined frame.

That's the difference between Harold and me: He believes in black and white, and thinks objective facts can save the world. Everywhere I look, I see subjective shades—and can't rest till I capture them somehow. Harold's closet is packed with sensible footwear; mine is overflowing with vintage cameras rescued from flea market bins.

But it seems to work with us, somehow. He always asks to see my photographs and paintings, and he's the reason I've embarked on my mission to watch every Jeff Goldblum movie chronologically, and then reverse chronologically. "If you're going to do something compulsively, at least apply a system to it," he said after I made him watch *Thor: Ragnarok* for the dozenth time. We work together, in a yin-and-yang way. Opposites attract, and all that.

But now academic merit is tearing us apart! For the entire summer!

Major bummer.

A flicker of warm white light floods the window. A string of twinkle lights have burst into life outside. They're new.

Harold looks up. "What's that?"

I stand and look outside, faking nonchalance. "What? The lights?" I shrug. "Dunno . . ." Watching him from the corner of my eye, I add: "Maybe you should check it out . . ."

Harold's eyes widen. I try (and fail) to suppress a smile. He's too easy.

Lots of people know that Harold is Mensa-level smart and the kind of socially active that means teachers call him "Mr. President"—and they aren't talking student council. But nobody else knows he's the biggest sucker for grand gestures this side of a Julia Roberts movie marathon. Nobody but me.

"What is it?" he asks again, a little-kid earnestness in his voice.

I throw my hands up. "Like I'm gonna say it now? Just go in the backyard and find out!"

Packing immediately forgotten, Harold flashes me a blinding smile and runs out of the room. I follow, bounding down the stairs—skipping the squeaky third step—and racing through the kitchen, where Harold's mom, Angie, is washing and wiping down every dish before putting them in the dishwasher. I barrel out the French doors.

Harold stands at the edge of the deck. Before him, on the broad expanse of beachy crabgrass, sits an igloo made of shoeboxes. A salt-tinged ocean breeze jangles the twinkly lights, darting uneven shadows across the yard. Harold's dad, Stuart, helped me string the lights from the house to the igloo and drape them all over the very DIY structure. It took days of testing in my own yard to be sure the structure would stand—with the help of plenty of superglue. Angie and Stuart made sure Harold would be gone all day while I sweated under the late-June sun, stacking box on box on box. But watching the igloo glow under slowly emerging stars, I can say with total certainty: It was worth it.

In California, the temperature plummets the moment the sun sets. Even as I shiver, I feel warmth radiating off Harold's skin. He's been obsessed with exploring the Arctic since he first watched a globe spin. He tracks shifts in Earth's polarity, and has read every book and watched every documentary about all those awful Arctic expeditions where men got lost and ate their dogs and then one another, all in the name of getting to the North Pole. Just to say they did. Harold is *into it*. He might be obsessed with facts, and science, and changing the world, but at heart he's a real romantic.

"Wow," he says, barely above a whisper.

I nudge his arm. "You can go in," I say. He looks at me like I am actually Santa Claus. I laugh. "Go!"

Harold leaps off the deck. He has to crawl on hands and knees to shimmy in. I can tell he's scared of bumping the igloo and sending it toppling. I don't bother to explain how much superglue is keeping the thing upright.

I follow after him, anticipation so intense it feels like neon's running through my veins. The igloo is big enough to fit two people, but just barely.

"Okay, lie down," I tell Harold while I crawl toward the back. He hesitates, looking around at how tiny the space is. "Just do it!"

He curls into the tiniest ball possible, to leave room for me. I grab a little black box that was hidden in the back of the igloo and set it by Harold's hip. "Close your eyes." I settle in beside him, flip the switch on the box, and lie back. We're side by side again, but it feels different when we're horizontal. I'm more comfortable, and more alert. The muffled air inside the igloo is charged.

"Open."

The box is a mini projector, and it throws video of the aurora borealis onto the arc of the shoebox igloo's ceiling. The waves of mystical Arctic light undulate like a disco ball refracting a rainbow. Stuart helped me build the igloo, but I kept this part a secret. This is just for Harold and me.

Harold takes in a breath. His body tenses for a second. Then he lets out a delighted yell that devolves into a laugh full of joy and wonder.

The fake borealis (fauxrealis?) casts the shoeboxes, the UC Santa Cruz fleece covering the ground, and our tightly coiled bodies in a multicolored glow. It's like we're inside a lava lamp. The igloo smells like dried glue, cardboard, and new-sneaker plastic. I feel bubbly, a kind of effervescence right under the skin. My body lights up at Harold's slightest shift.

"Wow. Ivy . . ." He turns his head and I'm scared to turn mine. To meet his eyes. We're so close—making eye contact right now would be like walking onto hot coals.

I do it anyway.

Harold's eyes are a slightly lighter brown than his skin. They're steady amid the waves of hectic light. A feeling comes over me— like when you dive into the ocean. Before cold or wet or the need for air kick in, there's one fraction of a second when the senses are so overwhelmed that everything is clear and painless.

Harold reaches out and grabs my hand, folding it in his. So warm.

"Thank you," he says.

The back door slams. I'm so startled that I sit directly up, bumping my head against the igloo ceiling.

"What's the big deal about this thing?" Stuart's voice booms. "What're those lights in there?" Harold sits up, too. We look at each other and start laughing, awkwardly. "Honestly, I don't understand it. Igloos? Is that what the youths are into these days?"

Harold drops his head into his hands and I almost fall over laughing. Stuart is a coding wizard and a self-made millionaire, but he's also the fatheriest father ever to be a dad. And it *is* funny, but this time Stuart did more than interrupt the principal during parent-teacher night. He disturbed . . . something. Whatever was happening between me and Harold a minute ago . . . I don't know. I've never felt something like that before, and definitely not for my best friend since fourth grade.

What *was* that??

There's no time to give Harold so much as a questioning glance, because he's crawling back out of the igloo to tell his dad about the surprise I planned for him. And in just a few hours, he'll basically be on the real North Pole for the summer, leaving me alone to figure out whether something just changed between us.

CHAPTER 2

It's been two weeks since Harold left. It's 10:00 a.m. and I'm sweating through my old Dora the Explorer sleeping bag and watching *Invasion of the Body Snatchers.*

It's official: Boredom has set in.

I'd be fully off my rocker if it weren't for VEIL, an art-sharing app I found out about the night Harold left. Users can post videos, images, words, gifs, whatever—without having to reveal their identities. But VEIL has taken the anonymous thing to another level: If you put up a selfie, its algorithm will blur your face; if you put up a text post, it'll black out proper nouns. It also only shows posts by users within five miles of your current location. Turns out, people will post *really* personal stuff when they know their name won't be attached. I've read some confessions, posted in the middle of the night, that would make a Real Housewife blush.

Then, every Sunday at midnight: *poof.* All the posts are gone. The feed gets completely repopulated starting Monday morning, and there's no way to save or share anything. The mandatory impermanence frustrates me sometimes, but I get it, in

11

a "we're all just specks of dust in a vast and endless void" kind of way. Thing is, it's still possible to figure out if multiple posts are from the same person. At least I think I've been able to identify a few pictures with notably similar composition (and telltale filter choices) as being from the same source. And some posts— like the ones where a poet uses limerick structure again and again, and the person who's providing daily updates on Sudden Cove's only black squirrel—are meant to form a pattern.

"Ivy! Are you up? Get up!" My mother never got the memo that people should talk more quietly in the morning. She only has one volume and it's high, because as a college professor, she has to be heard all the way in the back of the lecture hall. "Painted Lady Day waits for no teenager. We're gonna walk down now."

Mom and Dad have been worried about me since Harold left. I think I'm holding up quite well, all things considered, but they've decided to start including me in everything they do. Problem is, both my parents are professors of ecology at the University of California, Santa Cruz. Their idea of a good time includes documenting algae in tide pools or watching *Planet Earth* over and over. Never once did it occur to Mom or Dad to send me to art camp, which is where most of Belfry High's art punk crowd are spending their summers. No, I didn't ask. But still.

Thankfully, today is different. I love Painted Lady Day. It's a tradition started by the Sudden Cove Historical Society and spun out of control by the Ancient Mariners, a boating club that meets at the Calamity Clam Brewery down by the docks. Originally, the historical society wanted to find a way to honor the *Painted Lady*, a gigantic yacht built in the early 1900s and owned by Jon A. Arthur, an über-rich robber baron who sailed it from Sudden Cove to Baja and back every year. In every photograph and painting of Jon A.—and there are a lot of them around Sudden Cove, the man is a local icon—he's rocking a striped sweater and red beanie cap, like he's Old Hemingway and the Sea. Legend has it that before setting sail for the grand voyage, Jon A. would always go to Calamity Clam and buy a round for everyone, a tradition that came to be known as the "Sloppy Send-off."

Until one fateful year when Jon A.—mere miles from shore—suffered a heart attack at the wheel of the yacht. The *Painted Lady* capsized, Jon A. died, and the Sloppy Send-off was no more.

The historical society started Painted Lady Day as a beach-front barbecue, but the Ancient Mariners joined up with Calamity Clam to host a competition: Any group of two or more people can hand-make a vessel to brave the ocean waters out front of Calamity Clam. You win if you don't sink.

Harold and I have watched Painted Lady Day go down many times. Whenever one of us needs a pick-me-up, we send each other gifs of Ancient Mariners tipping overboard. I'd been avoiding thinking about the occasion because Harold isn't here to enjoy it with me. Then Mom announced her new grad student, Henrik, had entered the competition with some fellow TAs. So now I'm dressed in my most nautical of outfits, clutching my new Canon AT-1 camera, which I won on eBay a week ago, walking down the hill to Calamity Clam with a parent on each side.

There's already a bustling crowd of people at the Clam wearing blue-and-white striped sweaters and red beanies. Sand starts to mingle with loose asphalt under our feet. The salt air hangs in a thick marine layer of fog. The ocean's ever-present *whoosh* underlies the excited hum of chatter. Dozens of DIY boats are lined up in the parking lot.

"There's Henrik!" Mom points at a group of striped gentlemen standing next to a thin wooden boat with a carved dragon head on its prow. Henrik turns out to be about eight feet tall and violently blond—he's a legit Viking, and he carved this longship by hand. I rush through the hellos and get to shooting. The boat, and Henrik, and everyone wearing stripes, and the foggy light: photographer heaven! There's no way to take a bad photo on a day like today.

Snap snap snap. I grab picture after picture, making minute adjustments to the framing, and opening the aperture to wash out the color like an old Polaroid. I take a couple shots with my phone as well. Maybe I can post something to VEIL later.

"All right, they're about to start," Mom says. "We gotta get out of the way."

I take a couple more shots, then twist the Canon's lens cap back on. I don't have to ask where we're going—obviously we need to be on Calamity Clam's deck, watching the madness with mugs of hot cocoa in our hands.

Dad manages to get us a table where we have an unobstructed view of the crews hauling their boats across flat sand toward white-tipped waves.

"Oh, to be twenty years younger," Dad sighs. "I would build a boat from a hollowed-out tree."

Mom laughs into her mug. She pats him on the back. "Sure you would, hon."

Dad looks out to the water with longing. He came to Sudden Cove as an ecology grad student, and my mom was his advisor. They caused quite the scandal when they started going out, apparently, but now they're both tenure track at UCSC and are drawing national attention for building up the climate science post-grad program there. Between teaching, overseeing a research lab, and peer-reviewing dozens of articles every year, there's hardly time for Dad to plant a tree, much less hollow one out by hand.

My mom and dad are some of the smartest people I know. If they'd taken their jumbo-sized brains and studied corporate law or software engineering, we'd probably be one of those families with a brutally modern Sudden Cove vacation house. But instead they stuck to the school they loved and fought tirelessly for money to study rising sea levels. It's about the least sexy kind of science to study—it's hard to make people focus on the end of the world. But they fight and fight and fight. Even my dad, the king of the sarcastic comeback, gets red in the face when he lectures about shortsighted energy policies.

It's kind of adorable.

I wish I felt as passionately about tide pools and saltwater treatment plants as they do. When I attend rallies with them, my attention drifts to how to best capture the size of the crowd (fish-eye lens? panorama?), or whether black and white or color would be most appropriate to reflect the rally's tone. That's my parents, and Harold—saving the world, with me right behind them, recording the whole while. I suppose that's why it works with all of us.

"Well," Mom says, "if it's any consolation, you look *very* dashing in stripes."

Dad waggles his eyebrows.

I throw my head back. "Ugggghhhh." Having parents who love each other is so embarrassing.

I distract myself by firing up VEIL. When the feed populates, a chill runs through me, despite the sun breaking through the last bit of cloud cover. Intellectually, I knew that VEIL users were in Sudden Cove. But now, scrolling through pic after pic from Painted Lady Day, I can *feel* them around me. Who *are* they?

I look around, trying to detect anyone taking a picture with their phone, or see if anyone's screen is filled with VEIL's signature purple glow. Mom catches my eye and stares at me. This is a professor trick. It works; I put my phone away. She smiles. "Thank you."

"Did you get some good photos?" Dad asks.

I shrug. It's impossible to say till I get them developed. That's part of why I love shooting film. Photographs shape memory. With digital pictures, a moment is edited, enhanced, and filtered into rosy recollection. The elevated image becomes the version you remember. Film, on the other hand, is never pristine—it might be out of focus, or tilted a bit, or accidentally double exposed. But an imperfect photo echoes the flaws of the moment, and of memory—just one version of the truth.

Dad elbows me. "If you took up surfing, you could get shots from the water." Dad's dream in life is that I become a nature photographer. But I've watched the behind-the-scenes of *Planet Earth*. Waiting ten hours for some deadly snake to crawl your way? No thanks.

Mom frowns. We look more alike when we frown than when we smile. It is physically impossible to be mad at Veronica Warner when she's smiling—she has this great big grin with dimples and eyes that twinkle and the whole bit. I got her blond hair and athletic frame, but Frank Harrison's dark eyes, serious downward-curving lips, and penchant for wearing black. When we go places as a family, people treat my mom like she's been abducted by a morose cult.

"Surfing is dangerous," Mom says. "Especially with a bunch of idiots trying to manage unseaworthy vessels."

"Your grad student is one of those idiots!" Dad protests.

Mom shakes her head. "Yet another reminder that 'book smart' isn't the same thing as, well . . . smart in general."

Turns out, Mom's right. Henrik's Viking ship is gorgeous and intimidating, but it capsizes at the first wave. He and his crew drag the boat back to the parking lot, freezing and dejected. We watch while sipping our second round of cocoa. Dad barely hides his satisfied grin.

Later, I open the pictures I took on my phone. I thumb through filters and adjust brightness, saturation, and tone. But ultimately, for the millionth time, I close VEIL without adding anything. Contributing has always been my parents' thing, or Harold's thing—not mine. And there's already boatloads of people posting better images, anyway. Seems safer not to try.

CHAPTER 3

With Harold gone, my new best friend is Patton Malone, the hipster with round glasses and alopecia who owns Aperture Rapture. It's the only place in town that develops honest-to-god film, so I'm there a lot. Luckily Patton is pretty cool, and it's right next to Beach Reads, the bookstore I've been going to since I could crawl. Kristi, the owner, gets worried if I don't pick up my book-of-the-month in a timely manner. I wander the stacks while my film gets developed.

My first stop in Beach Reads is always the art book section, then comics and graphic novels, and then magazines. I love looking at the lush gardens and fine lines in *Architectural Digest*. Then I wander over into the tech and specialty section, digging for issues of *Shutterbug*. Today I'm distracted by the beaming face on the cover of *San Jose* magazine: It's Rake Burmkezerg, his strawberry-blond hair set off by a smattering of freckles. The headline reads: *Art to Table: The Local Art Movement Gets a Boost from VEIL*.

I grab the issue, flop down into the cracked leather seat of one of Beach Reads' massive armchairs, and flip to the Burmkezerg feature.

HOW A NEW PUPPY AND TIBETAN MONKS INSPIRED THE HOTTEST NEW SOCIAL APP

By: Danielle Feree

Let's face it: The last thing anyone needs is yet another app to share photos, videos, or text with their friends. In fact, it was while perusing Instagram that twenty-eight-year-old tech wunderkind Rake Burmkezerg had a revelation. "I was sick of seeing what my friends were posting," he says with a shrug. "You don't just see it once—my best friend got a puppy and I heard about it like twelve different ways. It made me tired. Strangers are a lot more interesting. I wanted someplace I could find new, unusual stuff that people around me were doing."

And when Burmkezerg says *"around me,"* he means it literally: VEIL is limited by geography. The app only shows users what's been uploaded within five miles of their current location. "Social media has allowed us to keep the same friends, regardless of where we are in the world," he says. "But what about your fellow grocery shoppers? The people who share your commute? The neighbor whose dog is always barking? I wanted to know what they're up to."

The problem with the age-old urge to spy on your neighbors? We're much more likely to *spy* than *share*. "People signed up, but they'd just lurk," Burmkezerg says. "We needed some greater incentive to post. That's when I thought about all the things I do in my house that I hope the neighbors don't see. I dance, I sing, I talk out loud to myself. I'm a pretty authentically odd person when I assume no one's watching. That's how I got the idea to make the app anonymous."

Turns out, a lot of people share Burmkezerg's curiosity. After launching this spring, more than half a million people have used VEIL. A massive success, measured against the company's internal growth plan. But the VC buzz or IPO rumor mill that typically accompanies that kind of expansion hasn't materialized. That doesn't bother Burmkezerg. "We weren't getting attention from New York or Los Angeles, or even here in San Francisco, because we diverted attention from those markets," he explains. "Some of our most active communities are places like Fayetteville, Asheville, Omaha. We want neighbors to connect with each other in a genuine way, rather than assuming someone in Topeka gives a crap about what a fashion blogger in Williamsburg is doing. Why should they care?"

Burmkezerg's commitment to anonymity defines the VEIL experience. Not only are users able to share unattributed content, they know their posts will vanish into the internet ether; every Sunday night, VEIL is wiped clean, and users are treated to an entirely new feed Monday morning.

When I ask Burmkezerg about the temporary timeline function, he sits up and leans over the table, nearly upsetting the hookah we've been sharing. He tells me about seeing a traveling troupe of Tibetan monks create a sand sculpture while he was studying at the University of Illinois at Urbana-Champaign. They were piecing together a mandala—a complex art piece of intertwining shapes and colors—one grain of sand at a time. "And then," Burmkezerg says, hands raised, eyes wide, "they just—poof—destroyed it." He wipes his hands to the side, once again threatening the stability of our hookah pipe. The point? "It was meant to demonstrate how fleeting life is. Everything we build can only last for so long."

Even VEIL?

"*Especially* VEIL," he says. "I built in what I call the self-destruct—the Sunday sweep—because I wanted our users to embrace the ephemeral nature of art, and life."

So, VEIL users: Let your freak flag fly. And don't worry. Anything you share will be gone Monday morning.

"There she is!"

I lower the magazine, jolted back to reality by Kristi's high-pitched greeting. She walks toward me, a stack of books in hand. There are no fewer than three pairs of glasses in the pile of silver-gray hair atop her head, and the linen drapes of her caftan swish around her feet. It looks like she's floating across the bookstore floor.

"Just got in a new biography of Ansel Adams that I set aside for you," Kristi says, placing her hand on my elbow and steering me to the front of the store. "Where is Harold? I haven't seen him in ages. There's a new book about quantum physics he just has to read."

Harold and I were beta testers for the personal book-matching program Kristi created a few years ago. The idea is you give the bookstore a sense of what you like to read, and leave payment on file. Each month one employee (usually Kristi) picks out a title they think you'd like. Pick it up, read, enjoy. Rinse, repeat! Kristi really racks her brain to find new and interesting things for Harold and me, and I never have to worry about what to read next.

"He's at Stanford for the summer," I tell Kristi as she glides behind the main counter. Jaz Clarke, a girl in my grade, sits at the ancient cash register. Jaz has a crown of kinky brown hair and a wardrobe full of brightly patterned maxi dresses I've always secretly envied. She just started working here this summer. Jaz gives me a slight smile, then ducks her head to look at her phone. Kristi launches into a mini rant about the number of books she's ordered for Harold this summer that she'll have to keep on the back shelf until he returns. I wince, biting back the urge to tell her that if anyone should be miffed at Harold's absence, it's me. I'm his best friend and he can barely find the time to send back a "things are going great!" text once a week.

While Kristi complains, I lean in to peek at Jaz's phone screen. Is she looking at what I think she's looking at? Judging by the faint purple light that spreads across her glowing brown cheeks, I think it's VEIL . . . And when I lean in a little farther, I confirm.

It's *everywhere*.

"Ivy?"

I glance up, blinking.

"Anything else, dear?" Kristi asks. She holds out the Ansel Adams paperback.

I grab the book and stuff it in my backpack, trying to calm racing thoughts. The article said half a million people are on VEIL—so many! And even people with a life and friends and a summer job, like Jaz Clarke, are on it. Being—how did Burmkezerg put it?—their most authentically odd selves. Is she the user who posts pictures of all the awesome vintage dresses they get at estate sales every weekend? Or the one who traces chalk outlines of their feet on every step of Sudden Cove's hidden staircases? She could be any of them.

"No, thanks." I smile, hoping Jaz didn't see me creeping on her tech. "See you soon," I tell them both, waving as I head next door to pick up my pictures.

Wind chimes over the door burst into a metallic chorus when I walk into Aperture Rapture. Since film isn't exactly the way to fame and fortune, Patton has stuffed his tiny store with more lucrative fare, like selfie sticks, frames, photography books, and gently used cameras. He's also replaced the stock photos in every single frame with shots of his Siamese cat, Orloff.

The wind chime cacophony summons Patton from the back room. "Ah!" Patton removes the yellow rubber gloves he uses for mixing chemicals and tugs a black beanie over his pale, bald head. "If it isn't Sudden Cove's very own Vivian Maier!"

"Its very own who, now?"

His eyes light up. "Who is Vivian Maier? Oh, you're going to love her." He strides into the store, making a beeline for the bookshelves. "She was a hidden gem, an unsung hero. She spent her whole life wandering the world, especially the streets of Chicago, basically inventing street photography."

"Like the Sartorialist?"

Patton lifts his nose up in the universal sign of snobbish dismissal. "The Sartorialist absolutely *wishes* he was Vivian Maier."

The wind chimes erupt anew as someone else enters the shop. I turn to see who it is, but they've disappeared behind a display of acid-free photo boxes. Patton finds the book he was looking for. The woman on the cover wears a wide-brimmed straw hat and holds up a vintage camera. It's a self-portrait, taken in a shopwindow. Vivian—it must be her—looks directly into the camera, almost challenging the viewer. She's a plain-looking woman with a sharp nose, but the composition of the photo (the sun hitting her face just so, the tilt of her hat, the city stretching out behind her, black and white and gray with grime) makes her look like a model.

No, better: like art.

"She was unknown and uncelebrated in her life," Patton says. "After she died, a collector accidentally ended up with boxes and boxes of her photos. Now she's shown at the best museums in the world." He returns to the counter. I linger, running a hand over Vivian's dark-eyed expression. "Your work reminds me of hers," he says, grabbing the basket of prints waiting to be picked up. "You have an eye for the light—black and white suits your style. Ah—here we are. Harrison, Ivy."

Oooooh boy. Patton's just compared me to someone whose art is good enough to be shown in museums and printed in books. I should be blushing with pride, but instead my stomach twists in a tight knot. I hope he hasn't looked *too* closely at my newest batch of photos, because they could throw a wrench into his whole fledgling-artist view of me.

I've started taking photos of my favorite VEIL posts.

A few weeks ago, someone began a day-to-day documentation of their chemotherapy treatments: wires, needles, and the mocking calm of the blue-and-white-patterned hospital gowns. I can tell it's the same poster because of the consistency of content, and framing, and filters. And another little detail that, for some reason, really breaks my heart: There's always a tortoiseshell backpack, crumpled in the corner or tangled in bed sheets. Come Monday mornings, after VEIL has reset, the tortoiseshell backpack user's posts are the ones I miss most.

Yesterday, one of those images hit me so hard I lost my breath. It was the crook of a brown-skinned elbow, riddled with needle pricks. Someone had connected the wounds with a shaky hand, creating constellations amid the rainbow discoloration of new and healing bruises.

I just couldn't bear to think that I wouldn't have that image in my life anymore. So I took a picture of it with the Canon and sent it in to be developed.

I don't know if Patton knows about VEIL, or has a strong stance on intellectual property rights. But I know I don't want to be busted for preserving pictures that are supposed to vanish forevermore. Here's hoping Patton is unhip or unscrupulous—or both.

I bring the book to the counter. Patton opens the envelope of my pictures and takes a couple out, setting them in front of me. One is a shot of an empty bench and vintage lamppost that sit on the jogging path that wends along the coast, just north of the boardwalk. A swirl of joggers, walkers, and bikers blurs behind the bench, which faces the ocean impassively, like always.

"See?" Patton says, spinning the picture to examine it again. "Beautiful."

Something moving behind me grabs Patton's attention. His eyes light up. "Candace!"

The other person in the shop has emerged from behind a display case. She's a brunette woman small enough to get lost in Patton's giant hug. She's wearing a long denim shirt, black leggings, and woven black sandals, hair tied up in a messy bun. Her eyes crinkle in a warm smile.

"Candace, may I introduce you to Ivy Harrison. Ivy, this is Candace Hubbard, the new art teacher at Belfry."

I draw myself up nervously. She's pretty young to be a teacher, but she *is* a teacher, so there's no way I'm going first-name basis. I've heard too many rants from my parents about the overfamiliarity of *kids these days.* "Hi, Ms. Hubbard."

"Oh, Candace, your photo boxes came in just yesterday, let me dig them out of the back." Patton disappears behind the black velvet curtain that separates the storage area and darkroom from the front of the store.

"So," Ms. Hubbard says, leaning against the counter. She's almost exactly my height, but something about the way she stands makes her seem way, way bigger. "You're into photography?"

"Yeah." I lift up the Canon hanging around my neck as a kind of feeble confirmation.

"And you're gonna take art this year?" She lowers her head and raises an eyebrow.

I shuffle my feet.

Last year's art teacher, Mr. Nguyen, was some kind of ceramics wizard. He barely paid attention in class and used up half the kiln for his own vases and mugs, which we found out he was selling on Etsy for like ninety-five dollars a pop. It was fine by me. Art was basically a free period where I sketched, researched old cameras, and spied on Loretta Kim and her crew of art punks. They all have home studios and are going to art school after they graduate and are brilliant and magical. I spent the year hoping to gain genius by osmosis. But then the administration caught wind of Mr. Nguyen's side hustle and he got the boot.

I hadn't planned on taking art again. But for some reason, in the face of Ms. Hubbard's tractor beam of confidence, I'm powerless to answer anything but "Yeah, of course."

"Great," she says, slapping her hand down. Her attention drawn to the counter, Ms. Hubbard reaches out to spin around the photos sitting there. I freeze while she examines them, my face and neck flaring volcano red.

"Hmm." Ms. Hubbard looks at me like I'm blurry and she's trying to focus. "May I see some others?"

I take the rest of the prints from the bag and set them out.

Patton reappears with a stack of black shrink-wrapped photo boxes and sets them on the counter. "Ooh, what are we doing? Finding her best shots?" Without hesitation, Patton points out a picture I took while dangling off the edge of Beachside Cliffs. The gray scale makes the sand look like a vast, unchanging sky, and the way the waves retreat leaves cloud-like wisps behind. It's an optical illusion, of sorts. It turned out even better than I'd hoped.

Watching Ms. Hubbard examine the photo makes me feel like a hundred tiny pins have all been pushed into my skin at once.

"Wow." Ms. Hubbard shakes her head, examining several of the prints. "This work shows so much promise. I'd be happy to assign special projects for you, to explore with photography."

I duck my head. "I'll think about it." I gather up my pictures, reseal the envelope, and hold up the book. "Can I . . . ?"

Patton waves me off. "Just take it and go, doll. I'll add it to your tab."

Outside, I lean against the bike rack and catch my breath. Mr. Nguyen's replacement just waltzed into my camera shop and offered to give me special assignments. I'm excited, I'm nervous, I'm flattered, I'm . . . sad. Because Harold should be here to celebrate with me. I want my best friend back. And I want an answer to just what in the heck that *moment* in the igloo really meant.

Something changed in the igloo. I planned, built, and sprung that surprise on him, and I know he loved it. But the fact that there's basically been radio silence since then has created this kind of . . . I don't know? Unequal footing? Anyway, I have the strong feeling that it isn't *my* turn to reach out.

To stave off overwhelming self-pity, I pull up VEIL. The screen fills with royal purple, then fades into a news feed crammed with pictures and text. For the hundredth time, I click the "create post" button. I point the phone's camera at my forest-green refurbished road bike—named Leibovitz, after famous photographer Annie Leibovitz—in the bike rack. The bike is covered in numbers scrawled in silver marker—pi to the zillionth digit. I lost a bet to Harold about the number of dead bodies that are still frozen on top of Mount Everest, and he won the right to decorate Leibovitz in the manner of his choosing. I added a compass, digital clock, and thermostat to the handlebars just to even out the dorkiness.

Next, I aim the camera at the shadow of a palm tree looming across the empty parking lot. At the reflection of myself in Aperture Rapture's blacked-out storefront, posing like Vivian Maier. But in the end I shut my phone off without posting anything. Like always.

I shove the phone, the Vivian Maier book, and the prints in my bag and climb onto Leibovitz. This moment feels like it could sum up my whole summer without Harold: antsy to be on the move, nowhere in particular to go.

CHAPTER 4

The antsy feeling persists, through weeks of random bike rides to take pictures around town, a handful of family outings to see nature documentaries at the San Jose IMAX theater, and dozens of Goldblum movies. On one endless late-August day, I am making my own entertainment. *Deep Cover* is on in the background while I position my phone on my desk to grab a shot of a VEIL post showing Monarch Park's playground equipment covered in knitwear. Standing on a chair, I squint into the Canon's viewfinder. The outline of the phone cover and the desk's wooden grain are visible in all my pictures of VEIL posts, but I kinda like that. The bloggers would call it mise-en-scène. Then, as I'm about to snap the shutter, a text bubble obscures the VEIL feed. I'm so startled, I nearly drop the camera. (What's the opposite of blowing up? That's what my phone's been doing all summer.)

It's a message from Harold:

2:13 p.m.
HAROLD
Guess who?

IVY
!!#@
really tho who this

HAROLD

IVY
JUST KIDDING YA GOOF
IM COMING OVER

The first thing I feel is relief. School starts *tomorrow*, and I was worried Stanford might have just asked Harold to stay for fall quarter. The second thing is a propulsive need to see my best friend. I knock over a pile of recently developed prints in my rush to throw on a hoodie, and barrel down the stairs. My parents sit on the couch cradling goblets of wine and laughing. It's the last day of summer for professors, too.

"Hey!" Mom says. "Where are you going in such a hurry?"

"Harold's back!" Mom and Dad cheer. I throw a quick "See you later!" over my shoulder, take off down the front steps, and leap onto Leibovitz.

My bike has made the ride to Harold's house so many times, it's basically its default setting. I try to concentrate on the gently swaying palm trees and the crisp wind to distract from a growing anxiety. Has Harold been running our igloo moment over and over in his mind, like I have?

His house always looks the same: yard freshly mown, flower beds neat and in bloom, porch swept and welcoming. The Johnsons made a mint when they sold their tech start-up—an app that tracks how many times you blink—to Big Eye Drops, and moved from San Jose to Sudden Cove with the hope of living slower-paced lives.

But it turns out you can take the overachievers out of the start-up, but you can't take the start-up out of the overachievers. Harold's mom and dad still work constantly, just from home offices. Their lives, and their house, are tidy and efficient. It's adorable when Harold talks a big game about being "way more chill" than his folks. Within the first week of freshman year, he'd signed up for seven clubs and was made president of three.

So chill. Pfft.

I lean Leibovitz against the driveway gate and knock on the front door, bouncing impatiently on my toes. No response. There's no text telling me *j/k, nevermind, come back later.* So I try the door. It's unlocked and creaks noisily when I shove it all the way open.

"Hello?"

Harold's voice rings out from the top of the stairs: "Come up!"

The house is quiet and feels empty. Must be office hours. I take the stairs two at a time. Harold's door is halfway open, and when I try to shove my way through, it runs up against a stack of books. Harold's sitting at his desk, which is also covered in books. Enormous paperback bricks with intimidating titles like *1600 or Bust* and *Research and Influence: Find You a University That Can Offer Both*. Most disturbing of all, his suitcase looks like it exploded upon impact with his bed. To Harold, the only thing better than going on vacation is coming home to unpack. If his room is any indication of his mental state, things are *not* good.

"Hey, buddy." I squeeze through the partially opened door.

Harold looks up from a gigantic tome. His eyes are bleary and half-focused, with dark circles underneath that were definitely not there when he left a couple months ago. He looks like he's Seen Some Stuff.

He leaps up and swallows me in a gigantic hug. "Hey," I say, relieved. He slouches back into the desk chair. I perch at the edge of his bed. "So. How was camp?"

He rubs his eyes, sighing. "Camp was . . ." Harold leans back. "Illuminating."

"Oh yeah?" I pick up another of the books, one so heavy it nearly breaks my arm. *You're So Behind and You Don't Even Know It: The Superior Teen's Guide to College Applications*.

"Everyone there was brilliant, Ivy," Harold says. He holds eye contact to make sure I'm really hearing him. "*Brilliant*. A thousand of them. All applying to the same schools."

"Well, that's okay. Aren't there, like, tens of thousands of institutions of higher learning in this country alone?"

Harold scoffs. "Yeah, but only a dozen worth considering."

I narrow my eyes. "Says who?"

With a broad sweep of his arm, Harold indicates all the books littering his floor. "Everyone!"

Uh-oh. Being around all those ambitious smarties has done a number on my best friend. He's always been the levelheaded one, the one who calms me down when I'm sure there's meat in the cafeteria's vegetarian options, or when I have an anxiety attack at the thought of opening a savings account. I was not prepared for this.

A light rap on the door announces Angie, who sticks her head in. She's wearing a black blazer with leather lapels. The Johnsons are the only people I know who wear business-casual at home. She's also matching her son's nervous energy.

"Harold—" Angie scans the room, her gaze stopping on me. And I might be imagining things, but I swear her mouth turns down ever so slightly. "Hey, Ivy. Harold, I left messages for the SAT tutors. I'll call the alumni associations tomorrow, okay?"

"Thanks, Mom," Harold says with a weak smile.

Angie lingers for a moment. "Don't hang out too long, okay? Gotta get ready for school tomorrow."

Now it's my turn to frown. I practically levitated on my way over here, and I can hardly believe that Harold is finally, finally back. But this isn't exactly the welcome-home celebration I had hoped for. Nodding at the atomic fallout of his suitcase, I ask: "Who are you and what have you done with

Harold Johnson? He'd never tolerate this Level Five domestic disaster."

Harold laughs. It seems to break a kind of spell. He jumps up and starts piling the clothes back into the suitcase. "How have you been?" he asks as he starts folding the discarded shirts. "How was your summer?"

How was my summer?

Excruciatingly boring.

Relentlessly tedious.

Unfathomably dull.

"Great," I say. "I got that Canon AT-1 and took a metric ton of photos."

"Ooh—any shots of someone actually using the tester lipstick at CVS?"

"I wish."

"What else?"

I experimented with my tolerance for volcano-hot Jim's Chips. Clarified the Urban Dictionary definition of "belch." Expanded my all-black wardrobe by at least seven dresses. Watched from *California Split* to *The Lost World: Jurassic Park*. I search my suddenly-very-empty mind for an answer, any answer, anything . . . What the heck else has been taking up my time for the last two months?

"Well, there's this app."

Harold looks at me over the red shirt he's folding that reads "The Science of Climate: There Can Only Be One." "An app?"

"It's called VEIL," I say. "It's sort of a secret thing? Like, people post things anonymously. Pictures or text or five-second videos or whatever."

"How is it anonymous?"

"I'll show you." I dig my phone out of my pocket. A purple glow fills my screen, and then: the stream. I show Harold the first few posts. One user shared a picture of a pile of books with the caption "lookit this freakin stack for ms ████'s class, was supposed to read like half by the end of summer lol yah rite." That's followed by a text post: "In May I swore that/They'd never take my freedom/First bell is death knell."

"Well, that's dramatic," Harold says.

"Right?" I say, beaming. "So great. And all these people are within five miles of us, right now. VEIL's algorithm thingy blurs faces and blocks proper nouns, to protect anonymity or whatever."

"So you don't know who wrote that?"

"Nope. But probably someone at Belfry."

"How do you know it's someone at Belfry? Couldn't it be anyone? Like a parent?"

"Gross. Don't even say that." I click the screen off and tuck the phone back in my pocket. "VEIL, like, *just* became a thing. I give it a good three months before the olds catch wind and ruin it."

"What have you posted?" he asks.

"Pfffft." I shake my head. "Nothing, obviously. Just wait till you see the level of stuff people are posting. There's no way anything I could come up with would compete."

"What?" Harold looks at me like I've lost it. "What about your pictures? Or your paintings?"

"Not good enough." I start scrounging inside my backpack to signal conversation: over. And maybe it's just that he's out of practice, but Harold completely misses the hint.

He tilts his head. "Seriously"—as though he's ever anything but—"at some point you have to start participating in your own life. This is like the fourth-grade science fair all over again."

I flinch, fiddling with the camera settings to avoid his gaze.

The fourth-grade science fair is a particularly painful memory. Not even Harold knows how painful. The project parameters were so broad that I was paralyzed and couldn't for the life of me come up with a good idea. Mom and Dad didn't want to help (something about "building character"). So I got a few disposable cameras and went with them on a research trip through Sudden Cove's many fields of tide pools. They were gathering samples for some study or another, and I took pictures of them filling vials, measuring salinity, and lecturing the few students who gave up their perfectly good Saturday to wade through brackish water with their teachers and their teachers' kid. So my project was basically cribbing my parents' real-life research to fill a trifold poster board, plus my original photographs. I got a B.

When my parents showed up for the science fair, they stopped at my booth for .05 seconds before beelining for Harold's exhibit on how community activists and scientists work together to raise awareness of major scientific issues and accomplishments. (To be fair to my parents, Harold drew a crowd: He had a megaphone and was holding up a protest sign.)

They talked to him for the entire show (Harold got first place) and invited him over for dinner. The hour I stood alone next to my project is still the single longest hour of my life.

Luckily, once Harold showed up at my house, he was happy to spend the entire time talking to me about *Avatar: The Last Airbender* like a normal pint-sized nerd. We've been best friends ever since.

And my parents framed my photos and hung them in our entryway.

"Yeah," I mumble, eager to move on from those memories.

Harold sighs and sits on the bed beside me, rubbing his eyes. I raise the camera and adjust the focus. Aiming my lens in Harold's direction, I press the shutter super fast. If I don't catch him candid, I'll just end up snapping pictures of his protesting hand. He isn't much for posing. He looks down the barrel of the lens and groans. "Just don't go putting that on VEIL."

"They'd blur your face anyway—anonymous, remember?" I lower the camera. He doesn't look convinced. "Okay, I promise. Film will stay IRL."

Harold grins. "I missed you this summer."

My smile back is strained. The last three months were a mishmash of dyeing all my shirts the exact same shade of black, watching nature shows with my parents, and taking photos of all the abandoned shoes I found on my long, lonely bike rides through Sudden Cove. Harold has no idea how much I mean it when I say, "I missed you, too."

CHAPTER 5

My parents take me out for a pancake breakfast at Bob's Flapjackery in the morning, a first-day-of-school tradition that no amount of growing up seems able to shake. (Then again, I hope I never get too old for churro waffles with extra whipped cream.) Afterward, they drop me and Leibovitz at school on their way to the university.

That means I'm at school way, way earlier than is customary or desired. I'd prefer to get rocket-blasted into my first-period class *just* as the bell rings. Less time to sit, alone and uncomfortable, while everyone else meets up with their friends and talks about how wonderful their summers were. My 911 text to Harold (*at school early, pls pls plllllssss tell me you are already there & waiting for me w/hot cocoa*) was greeted by dead silence.

Belfry High is on the inland side of the Pacific Coast Highway, nestled in a grove of white-barked eucalyptus trees. It's an open-air campus with pee-yellow stucco walls. All the buildings branch out from the central quad and are connected by covered corridors. The quad is a big grassy area between the cafeteria and the library where everyone gathers before school and during lunch.

I head toward one of the quad's plastic picnic tables and watch the kids stream in. Most of the faces are familiar, though I doubt any one of them could conjure my name. I realize a beat too late that I'm in the path of the boys' lacrosse team. They're the untouchable gods of Belfry High and I'm about to be trampled under their golden cleats. Elbows, shoulders, and washboard abs jostle me. Then—with nary an "oops, sorry"—they're gone, and with them my hopes of being even marginally less invisible this year.

Harold says my status as outcast is a self-fulfilling prophecy, based on my all-black outfits and resting Goth face. I told him it isn't my fault if everyone besides him is blind to my aura of awesome.

I avoid making eye contact by scrolling through the fresh VEIL stream. Audrina Lord has already posted a picture of her first-day-of-school outfit—a bright red poplin dress that no one is likely to miss. I know it's Audrina because she's one of the handful of users who spend all their time trying to game VEIL's anonymity system, writing her own captions on a whiteboard, or on her arm, leg, or other exposed body part.

Audrina and users like her make me sad. It's like they're allergic to the idea of posting a picture just for the sake of putting beauty into the world. The dopamine rush of getting upvotes (she already has more than a hundred, just for a poorly lit shot of a dress—*snooze*) is more important to them.

I prefer to scroll down the feed to the pictures with fewer upvotes. Those truly anonymous VEILers have become a strange little community. Some new posts are already up: There's one from the person who always captures sunrise from a surfboard, and one of my favorite posters of daily affirmations: "If a Girl Scout cookie can get more delicious in the fridge, you can get through the first day of school."

Does it make sense? No. Does it give me just enough of a boost to shut my phone down and walk to first period? You bet.

As I walk the D wing to my first class, I can't help but notice people staring down at their phones, the screens blaring a bright purple. Everywhere I look kids loiter, checking VEIL. I wonder which posts they're upvoting—Audrina, or the person who has added one rock per day to the overgrown patch of grass that is O'Connor Park, waiting for the city to notice?

Knowing that VEIL users like that walk the halls of Belfry High gives me hope for tenth grade. Maybe the dude struggling with his bike lock is the person who draws weekly cartoons about ornery, foul-mouthed redwoods. Or the person waiting in line for undercooked chimichangas could be the poster who writes poetry about Zendaya so beautiful it makes me cry. And somewhere in the crowd could be the person who drew GPS coordinates in sidewalk chalk on street corners all through the U.S.

When the lunch bell rings, I start biting my nails. Last year, Harold mapped the social strata of the quad at lunch like a true scientist: Seniors sit in the middle, the part of the lawn that's sunken down and lined with cement benches. Some juniors are honorary seniors, so they can get away with hanging mid-quad. But most of the eleventh grade sits in front of the entrance to the cafeteria, in the shade of the overhang. Sophomores get the patio by the library, partially shaded by oak trees. They sit on the plastic benches that stick to your legs when it's warm. And freshmen— ohhh, freshmen. They get the steps that run the whole southern half of the quad—no benches, no shade, and no warning when the seagulls get into V-formation to ritualistically empty their bowels.

Harold and I spent every lunch period last year sitting on the far end of the steps. We would observe and snark on everyone around us, or—more often—Harold would do homework and I'd flip through the most recent *Fortean Times* or work on some Goldblum sketches.

I'm happy to be moving to the patio this year. But when I approach the benches, Harold is nowhere in sight. I lean against the library wall and take my phone out, squinting at the blank screen. No textsplanation from my absent buddy. Part of me is actually concerned that something might be wrong.

11:13 a.m.

I V Y

Where you at?

11:15 a.m.

I V Y

Remember in that mission impossible when tom cruise is
hanging from a cliff

That's my situation here w/o buddy

Mission: lunchpossible

No response. Not even so much as an ellipsis bubble. I start
to feel my chest shrink and my breath go shallow. There's no way
to convince me that every pair of eyes in all of Belfry—maybe
in this entire postal code—isn't fixed on me right now, won-
dering, "Who is this loser eating lunch *all alone*?" I can't stand
in the heat and pretend not to be humiliated anymore. Trying
to be calm and casúal, I make for the library doors and duck
inside.

The library isn't the worst place to be forced to watch the
clock for forty minutes, all things considered. The tables are
packed with overachieving juniors with PSATs to study for and
seniors with college essays to write. It's all right to disappear here.

I just didn't think my best friend would leave me hanging
like this. There has to be a good reason. I mean, Harold was the
one who remembered to pass me a note between second and

third period every single day last year (most of the time asking for help with crossword puzzle clues). That isn't the kind of person who willingly abandons someone to the humiliation of lunching solo.

But when the bell rings, I still haven't heard from him.

Luckily, art is next. Even though I hadn't been planning to take it as my elective this year, I have to admit I'm excited. The classroom fills me with relief. It's as much a misfit as the students it houses: Seating is a mix of disused science lab tables, half-broken desks, and Costco fold-out tables that disappear every time Key Club holds a lunchtime donut sale. Though the room's ventilation windows stay propped open, it always smells like formaldehyde (from paint) and chlorine (from cleaning paint).

And, this year, there's Ms. Hubbard.

"Ivy!" Ms. Hubbard grins widely when she sees me. I'm shocked she remembers my name. "How was the rest of your summer?"

"I got a couple new cameras," I say hopefully.

"Oh, great," she says. "What else? Did you have any adventures? Get arrested? Or kissed?"

I tense up. Watching several decades of Jeff Goldblum films didn't exactly get me any closer to danger, or a swoony romance. The biggest adventure was that moment in the igloo with Harold, which has apparently been forgotten in a frenzy to get into an Ivy League school.

"Um, not really," I say. "I read a bunch about street photography."

"Wow—you're focused." She cocks her head. "Too bad we don't have a darkroom so you can develop your pictures properly."

I shrug. "It's okay, I got a club card at Aperture Rapture. I've almost earned a free Mapplethorpe fridge magnet."

"Well!" She claps her hands. "Let's hope this year holds some new thrills, shall we? Never forget: Life begets art. To create your best work, you have to have something to art about."

"Sure." I think of all the VEIL posters in my midst and, with renewed confidence, add: "It definitely will."

I grab the old lab table with the wonky leg against the far wall, my seat for all of last year. The best place to observe others without them seeing me. People start to drift in. I take out my sketchbook and a spanking-new pack of charcoal pencils. The seat next to me goes unclaimed—no surprise there. The invisibility force field I project is so strong, people probably can't see me, or the empty stool beside me, or this table.

Whatever. All the better to spy on you, my dears.

Just as the bell rings, my phone buzzes.

So sorry!!!! Harold writes. *Last-minute student council mtg @ lunch, had to nominate new treasurer. Sara Sussman spent her summer selling weed so she got probation & a demotion.*

Escandalo!!!! I write back. As juicy as that gossip is—and as relieved as I am to hear from Harold—the text in some ways sharpens my annoyance. He couldn't have sent a heads-up once it became clear I was being abandoned on the first day of school?

I tuck my phone away. Though the bell has rung, the noise level shows no signs of waning. Almost everyone here took art last year, and Mr. Nguyen never bothered to prepare "lesson plans," or to pay attention to the "schedule." He was kind of just *there*.

Ms. Hubbard leans against the desk, taking note of each of us, one by one. Slowly, everyone falls silent. Still our new teacher stands, arms crossed, staring. Eventually, the art punks are the last left chattering. We can all clearly hear Jeanne Romanoff recounting, in excruciating detail, her romantic dalliance with a ceramicist at her fine arts camp in the Catskills. Finally Loretta elbows Jeanne and the art punk table lapses into the same expectant quiet as the rest of the room.

Ms. Hubbard pushes off the desk to stand straight. She's all of five foot nothing, but her dark brown eyes and thin-set mouth project an aura of Big Boss.

"So." Her eyes sweep the room. "I'm Ms. Hubbard, the new art teacher. Please, call me Ms. H. It seems some of you have an extracurricular commitment to art"—Jeanne blushes—"but I don't want to assume anything about each student's level of experience or natural talent. So the first three weeks or so of this class will be based on assignments that will show me where you're all at. From there, I'll be able to further customize group and individual assignments, and determine where we should focus our time in the art history portion."

Wha? Group *and* individual assignments? Art history?? This is definitely not sounding like Mr. Nguyen's easy-A extravaganza. Everyone else is thinking the same thing. Jason Dimichek and Megan Matson huddle together, conferring in a worried hush.

Ms. H continues: "Ultimately, art is something you do, not something you teach. I'm here to answer questions, to guide you in the medium of your choice, and to push each of you to broaden your horizons as creative people."

The door squeaks open, cutting her off.

And in

walks

Hunky Nate Gehrig.

That's Hunky Nate Gehrig of Tag-and-Nate, twin brothers and starting wide receivers for the Belfry football team. The football team gets short shrift—they have to use the field on Saturday mornings because the lacrosse team plays on Friday nights—but the Gehrig brothers are still a big deal. Mostly cuz they're hot and tall. Like sexy cactuses.

Or something.

Deer have never looked at headlights as gape-mouthedly as I stare at Nate freaking Gehrig in this moment. At how his green

T-shirt clings to his sun-kissed biceps as he unfolds a note. At his dark hair, which flops oh-so-casually over his hazel eyes while he explains about accidentally being assigned a sixth period when obviously he has to be at football practice, so he's changing his whole schedule and does she have room for him in this class? I perish in the reflected light of his toothy smile when Ms. H says, "Yeah, sure." And then (AND THEN) Ms. H looks up with this twinkle in her eye like Halloween came early and she points right at me (RIGHT AT ME) and says, "Have a seat next to Ivy."

Trout have never flopped as air-gaspingly as my insides do while Nate Gehrig walks, as if in slow motion, to take the stool next to mine. My mind goes so blank I probably reach some highfalutin level of Buddhist enlightenment.

Nate Gehrig sits.

I stare straight forward, hardly breathing, while he takes out an oddly fancy notebook with a gleaming gold triangle on the cover. He runs his hands through his perfect, silken hair. Every muscle in my body is tense—I'm in a state of crush-induced rigor mortis. Every second we go without acknowledging each other builds a tension so thick I can only take tiny, wheezy breaths. I blurt out the only thought that's managed to worm its way into my brain:

"So, are you, like, in the Illuminati or something?"

Nate Gehrig looks at me with sheer confusion.

Dear god. Why. Why why why am I this person, why is this my mouth and why were those my words, and why isn't the roof of this building caving the hell in already so I can be free of this mortal cage of mortification?

"What's the Illuminati?" Nate asks.

Wait—what?

"Wait—what?"

"Yeah. What is that?" Nate asks, still looking at me like I have a third eye. But now I'm giving him the same look in return.

"The Illuminati." I point at the gold symbol on his schmancy notebook. "The group of elite people rumored to be secretly running the world? That's their symbol." I pause. "Allegedly."

Nate narrows his eyes. "Secretly running the world?"

"Yeah. Do you really not know this? Some people think they're lizard creatures from outer space."

This time the silence between us is heavy, but in a different way. "I really didn't," Nate says. "And I stole this from my brother, Tag, so guess I'm gonna have to ask him some questions."

Wait—was that a joke? Does Hunky Nate Gehrig have a sense of humor, on top of perfect hair and *Tiger Beat* eyes?

"I'd start with the secret society thing," I say. "The lizard stuff is best in follow-up."

Nate laughs.

I MADE NATE GEHRIG LAUGH.

"Good tip." He holds his hand out. "I'm Nate."

My entire hand disappears in his grip. His skin is rough and warm.

"Ivy."

Looks like Ms. H's prophecy about exciting things is already coming true. Maybe tenth grade won't suck so bad, after all.

CHAPTER 6

The flip side of the breakfast flapjack tradition is the uncomfortable scene that awaits me when I get home. My parents sit on the living room couch, eyes shining as they ask that inevitable question:

"How'd it go?"

I trudge into the living room and sink into our lumpy corduroy armchair. It molds to my body as I consider how to answer. How *did* today go? Even I am surprised when I answer: "It was good."

"Oh, thank god!" Mom says, relieved. Mom and Dad are the type who excelled at school without trying. Grades and gold stars mean a lot to them—I mean, they both stayed in school long enough to get PhDs, and even then they couldn't make themselves leave. They'll be in school their whole lives, *by choice*. They're both one banana shy of a flambé, if you ask me. Though they try hard to understand, they can't relate to how little I care about school. How I find it a chore to show up every day, when I know there's a whole world outside stuffy classrooms and carefully edited textbooks.

"Do you have any classes with Harold?" Dad asks.

I sigh. It's like he has a psychic laser beam into my mind; that's the one question I didn't want to answer. "No. I think they made him principal." I stare at the ceiling. "I'm not sure when I'll see him."

All summer I fought runaway imaginings of what it would be like if Harold came back from camp and said, "I've been thinking about our moment in the igloo, and . . ." I came up with a hundred ways for him to end that statement. Half of them broke my heart, the other half sent it racing.

Never did I imagine that he would come back and ignore it entirely, in favor of being secretary for the 4-H Club. I don't know how to feel, and honestly, I'd rather not think about it. Because, while giving my parents a positive spin on school is part of a tradition, so is calling Harold afterward and actually getting into it. Which teachers spent the summer going to yoga retreats, or getting a divorce; which students came back to school tall, or out, or with a nose piercing.

If he couldn't even shoot me a warning text at lunch, how is he going to make time for gossip calls?

After giving Mom and Dad the appropriate amount of face time, I retreat upstairs. My room's the only one on the second floor—it's in a finished attic, and it feels like a fancy treehouse. Early in the summer, I got permission to repaint every wall of my room a pure white. Then I draped twine between nails, making cute clotheslines on the walls on which to hang dozens and dozens of prints. Above the desk are a series of shots I got of Harold when he dressed up like an Elbow's Temple gnome for Halloween last year. Over the bed are psychedelic pictures of ocean waves taken with the help of a kaleidoscope lens Harold built one day when he was bored. Strung beside the recessed reading nook are several prints of the back of Harold's head at the peak, death drop, and G-force curve of the Big Dipper roller coaster on the Boardwalk. Somehow, you can tell what face he's making just from his ears. I swear.

He's inescapable.

Throwing my bag down, I fall backward onto the bed. Even that isn't safe: A poster on the ceiling depicts the position of the stars at the time I was born. A gift from Harold while he was going through an astronomy phase in eighth grade.

Okay, universe. I get it. Digging my phone out of my pocket, I flip on my stomach and open the texts, dashing off a quick note: *So, Mr. Dufrane's new Porsche. He had an interesting summer of selling his soul to the devil, I know it.*

The DELIVERED! note pops up, but no sign of a response from Harold. And he is literally the last person on earth who would turn on read receipts. With a sigh, I turn to my new constant: VEIL.

A rush of serotonin floods through me when the app's purple load screen boots up. The first image is a close-up of a black-and-white bunny face, with a little pink nose. This must be the user who's been documenting their rabbits all summer, including putting the bunnies in a state fair competition. How a judge could possibly rate one bunny more adorable than another, I'll never know, but that picture warmed my heart for a week solid.

Another post is from a poet who always writes in the same style:

F or some
I t's a prison,
R eturning after
S ummer truly
T orture. But not me. School's a

D aily escape,
A place to be safe, when
Y ou can't expect to

B e understood at home.
A t school, some
C an be themselves and
K now home's a world away.

I've spent the summer witnessing this poster get better at, and braver with, their poetry. Now, here's confirmation that the poet goes to Belfry, and they see it as a sanctuary. I let out a grunt of frustration. If only I could figure out who the poet is, I could join them in whatever safe space they've carved out at BHS.

Then I scroll to the next image.

A gasp catches in my throat. I nearly drop the phone.

**CAN'T BELIEVE LUKE HAAS DIDN'T GET HELD BACK
WE ALL KNOW HE GOT TREATED BETTER AFTER HE "CAME OUT"
GUESS BEING A HOMO MAKES UP FOR BEING DUMB AS A BOARD.
PROLLY THAT OR OFF HIMSELF LOL
SMH. JUST WHAT THESE FRUITCAKES NEED, MORE
ENCOURAGEMENT TO BEG FOR ATTENTION**

I blink—again, then again—to confirm the post is real. In the middle of the competitive bunny-raiser, the poet, the squirrel enthusiast, the person who records themself reading nutrient labels with a voice modulator, there's also this. This . . . Neanderthal.

Actually, that's insulting to Neanderthals. This is a moss-covered cretin who got lost on his way to 4chan befouling my beloved app, trying to make VEIL as coarse and hurtful as the worst parts of high school.

After spending months obsessing over VEIL regulars who share the beautiful mundane of our sleepy coastal lives, I felt like we'd formed a benign and gentle bond. Even the Audrina Lords have their own kind of charm.

It has never, ever, not even once, come close to being something like . . . this. Beyond bad—ignorant, hateful.

I turn off my phone and roll onto my back. The post hangs around me like a bad smell. I find myself wishing I knew everyone who posted to VEIL, so I could find out who posted that, sneak up behind them, and pop a balloon when they least expect it. Or put their hand in warm water when they fall asleep in class.

Or call the cops.

Ugh. Even the thought of that—of authorities invading our little art oasis—makes my stomach knot.

What was it that Burmkezerg said about remaining anonymous? That it would let strangers share the secret parts of themselves?

Sadly, not everyone's secrets are harmless.

CHAPTER 7

The next morning, my dreams have barely faded before my mind jumps to the post from last night. I scroll through VEIL with still-bleary eyes. No, the homophobic post was not a nightmare. It's there. And it's just as much of a kick in the gut reading it a second time.

I want to blow it off. People being dumb on the internet? Not exactly new. But the tone of the post . . . The way it assumes people reading it will somehow agree, or be remotely interested in what this criminally dunderheaded jerkwad has to say . . . And the fact that this person didn't just say this on ~the internet~. They said it on VEIL.

It lingers like a stubbed toe.

And apparently I'm not the only one who feels that way. The app is crammed with posts on the homophobic rant. There's no way to thread in the VEIL timeline, and usually VEILers are delightfully non-referential. It's a meme-free zone.

But people are *not happy* about the bigoted jerk.

Some have uploaded selfies of themselves giving the middle finger. Their faces and one-finger salutes are blurred beyond recognition, but the sentiment is clear.

Some have written text responses.

Is VEIL gonna kick the anti-gay bozo out of our art parade?

Homophobes to the left. Way far to the left, like even farther, like off-a-cliff left.

Who has two thumbs and one fewer social media app after this disaster? This guy.

The idea that one hateful post could drive beautiful geniuses off VEIL entirely, thus making the app worse for everyone—it makes me sick. I throw on an outfit that's even more black monotone than usual.

At Belfry, something *feels* off. It isn't like the open hallways of BHS are ever the pinnacle of calm and order, but today seems particularly chaotic. The buzz of conversation is louder, the furtive glances more targeted and lingering. I catch snippets of conversation as I move from class to class.

". . . Jay Kwan took a screenshot and . . ."

". . . got a text about it before I even opened VEIL, what the . . ."

". . . well, *someone* showed their parents. My dad was furious and . . ."

Even though I understood that people knew about VEIL, it's disconcerting to hear it on everyone's lips. The app's suddenly caught in the spotlight, all because of some degenerate troll's brain pus.

As the day goes on, the scandal reactions split into two camps: those asking whether the post should be removed or reported, and those arguing for the right to free speech, and noting Burmkezerg's goal of making the app a place where anything goes.

I get the free speech argument. I do. But I hate knowing that people I care about are feeling sad and hurt. And the thought that the post is being shared with people who don't even *get* VEIL (parents?! ugh) adds another layer of anxiety.

I get to Ms. H's class early. The door's open, but she's nowhere to be found. Loretta and Jeanne, however, are already in their seats, huddled close together. Ducking my head, I march to the back and make a big show of taking out my notebook. But, duh, I am eavesdropping on Loretta and Jeanne's conversation, hard-core.

"I just didn't realize the acrylic was so toxic. I thought I got the organic kind," Jeanne says. She holds paintbrushes spread out like a fan. The brush tips are stiff with dry red paint. Jeanne is clearly distressed.

The baby-blue curve of the brush's handle catches on something in my memory. I've seen brushes like that before on—what else?—VEIL. There's a poster who spent the summer doing daily flash paintings. Photos of the paintings were like something out of a hipster home catalogue, all light wood backgrounds, gentle afternoon lighting, and peach-toned carpets. Fanned out beside the artwork, usually, were a half-finished iced coffee, a pair of reflective sunglasses, and a few of these fancy-schmancy paintbrushes.

"Can Karen send you any more?" Loretta asks. Feeling the bristles, she accidentally snaps it off entirely.

Jeanne turns a queasy shade of green. She shakes her head. "Study abroad ended last week. She's already headed back from Seoul." Defeated, she sets the brushes down on the table. "I guess I can just use my crappy backup set. I don't know, I wasn't even sure if I wanted to keep doing those dailies. And now that stupid post? Maybe this is a sign."

Loretta pats Jeanne on the shoulder. "We'll figure something out."

People begin trickling into class, and Ms. H follows. Fellow art punks Jason and Megan join Loretta and Jeanne and the conversation shifts. But I zero in on the paintbrushes still peeking out of Jeanne's rumpled JanSport.

Reading and rereading that awful VEIL post and feeling tension vibrate through the halls of Belfry today have me feeling helpless. Like there's nothing I can do to make even one person feel better.

Until now. Now that I've serendipitously stumbled on the identity of a VEIL user—along with a problem very much in need of a solution. If Jeanne gets her brushes (if, say, some anonymous donor gave her a new set), she'll keep doing the daily paintings. Those daily paintings are part of what makes VEIL feel joyful. So if $A = B$ and $B = C$, then I think I can give Jeanne an anonymous gift and basically save VEIL. That's just math.

Right?

Plus, Burmkezerg's mission for the app, and his militancy about protecting anonymity, was all before VEIL included hate speech.

More than anything, though, is the fact that I *want* to help Jeanne so badly. It still makes me vaguely nauseous to think of posting to the site itself—surely no one would upvote it, and even if they did, it'd just be out of pity. But this concrete act of kindness for Jeanne seems like something I can do—something I can control—that benefits VEIL as a whole.

Nate tosses his backpack on the ground between us. "What's up?"

"Oh. Nothing." I shake my head while he perches on the stool next to mine. He's so tall the seat is short to him. Meanwhile, I have to leap up on them like they're lifeguard towers.

"You look happy."

"You say that like I'm always *un*happy." I frown.

"There!" Nate points at my face. "That's the usual look. You know—angsty. I thought that was your thing."

I stare daggers.

He smirks. "But really, what's up?"

Nate Gehrig and I have been high school classmates for one year, and he has known my name for, like, two seconds. But there's something about him that feels easy, like I can trust him to know where my sideways train of thought is going. I've only ever had this instant friend connection with Harold. But what I want to tell Nate now—about my plans to surprise Jeanne—could be taken about a hundred wrong ways. I can't trust him that much. Yet.

My frown deepens.

Nate spirals into laughter. "See? You can't help it."

"Fine. Fine! I have angst."

Ms. H is leaning against her desk, her silent call to attention. I lower my voice.

"But for the record, I prefer the term 'ennui.'"

Nate rolls his eyes. *"Bien sûr."*

Butter has never melted as baguettedly as I do when I realize: *Nate Gehrig speaks French.*

The gods are testing me.

I V Y

hiiiiiiii

H A R O L D

Heyy

I V Y

oh good I was worried id wake you up

H A R O L D

Pshaw

I've been up doing PSAT flashcards since 5:30

I V Y

😱

H A R O L D

Long time no text

I V Y

long time no SEE!

whose fault is that?!

H A R O L D

🙂

I V Y

make it up to me today

drive me to Monterey

HAROLD
Aquarium?

IVY
oooooo
Not what I was thinking but I like where your heads at
actually need to get s/t @ an art supply store there
for a secret project
thing

HAROLD
Let me get this straight.
You've got some crazy idea in your brain & it requires
driving somewhere
So you text to get me to haul your butt halfway down the
central coast
& you're not even gonna tell me what the project/thing
is?!?!?!??!?

IVY
. . .
yep

HAROLD
Cool.
Give me 15 to get dressed & I'll pick you up

CHAPTER 8

I flounce downstairs and find both parents in the kitchen. Typical Saturday chez moi: Mom arranges lilies in a vase and Dad reads the *New York Times*. He says he likes getting ink on his hands (ew). Mom says she likes how he looks wearing his thick-rimmed reading glasses (EW).

"Hey!" I grab a lime LaCroix from the fridge. "Harold and I are going on an excursion to Monterey."

Mom and Dad glance at each other, communicating silently. "Harold, huh?" Mom asks, trying to be nonchalant. Like I didn't just witness that little parental confab. "Haven't heard from him in a while."

"Yeah, when is he gonna come back around?" Dad carefully avoids eye contact and rattles the Style section. (He loves telling me about when he wore today's trends *back in the day*.) "We're doing another sample-collecting session in the hills over by Scotts Valley in a couple months. I want to give Harold the first chance to sign up."

"What!" I slam the fridge door. "You don't want to let *me* sign up first?"

Dad peers over the top of the paper. "Do you want to sign up first?"

"Pfft. No." I pop the LaCroix tab and take a fizzy sip.

Dad rolls his eyes.

"Well, just let Harold know he's welcome to come over anytime," Mom says. "We'd love to hear how camp went." I roll my eyes. Mom raises an eyebrow. "Not well?"

"I don't know. He came back panicked about college and hasn't even talked about how camp went. He joined every single club on earth and I've hardly seen him."

Mom frowns.

"Tell him to take it easy," Dad says from behind a wall of ink. "People love to get kids all worked up about what school they go to. Studies show that home environment and personal drive are much more important to academic achievement than anything else, and Harold's got those in spades." Dad turns a page. "But also tell him about the sign-up. Spots will go fast!"

"Sure." I give Mom a hug and grab my bag from the hook by the hall closet. "Later!"

Harold got his driver's license before anyone else, because he's a little old for our grade. When he passed, his parents said he could use the old VW Golf that'd been sitting in the back of their garage for as long as I could remember. Harold keeps the Golf meticulously clean; he has pride in his ride. Once, we went to the drive-in to watch *The Life Aquatic* and I put my feet up on the dashboard. The look that Harold gave me could've sliced diamonds.

But today when the Golf pulls up in front of my house, its passenger seat is covered with yet more reference books, and some pamphlets ("So You Want to Stage a Film Festival" and "The Truth About Mock Stock Club"). Harold smiles at me from the driver's side and just like that I'm transported back to the igloo, when lightning crackled between his skin and mine. His smile has always had the power to make me feel more awake, more comfortable—more alive. Harold Johnson: human espresso shot.

Then his smile falls as he scrambles to toss all the stray paperwork to the back seat. "Sorry, sorry," he mutters.

"Did your backpack explode in here?" I jump in and shut the door, then tug the handle halfway in so it'll stay shut. The Golf is one of those cars that have special tricks. I know them all.

"I've started to read in here. When I get home from school," Harold says.

"Why?"

He shrugs, turning to the road. "The garage is quiet. No one bugs me in there."

I face the road and try to sound casual. We merge onto the 1, a highway bordered by peeling eucalyptus trees, soaring desert palms, and the cloud-like branches of the red firs. "My parents are all tizzied cuz they haven't seen you. They wanna know how camp went."

"I miss those guys." Harold lets out a long sigh, leaning his head back against the car seat headrest. "Where am I headed? And what is this project?"

I open the directions on my phone and angle it in the cup holder so he can keep an eye on the map. "Well, it's kind of a VEIL thing."

"Hmmmm."

"Don't *hmmmm* VEIL," I say, a little more sharply than I intended.

"Well, now that I know it's a site where people post anti-gay sentiments . . ."

"Ugh. You heard about that?"

"Yeah," Harold says, sounding offended. "We talk about a lot more than reseeding the softball field during student government, you know."

"News to me." I fiddle with the window lever in the passenger side door. "VEIL isn't like that. Usually. That was an outlier."

"Well, they aren't doing anything about it, either," Harold says. It's obvious he has strong feelings about this. "They need to take responsibility. Burmkezerg. VEIL. Someone."

I sigh. I don't even disagree with Harold, not really, but he's missed the part where this exact argument has been raging on VEIL for the last forty-eight hours. And, okay. Maybe there's a little pang of annoyance that Harold's talking about VEIL like he's an expert, when I seriously doubt he's even had the time to download it. "If they delete the post, what's to stop them from deleting anyone else's post? For whatever reason?"

"Come on, Ivy. That was hate speech. VEIL—Burmkezerg—should be able to differentiate."

That's fair.

"And," Harold continues, "arguably they could do something more effective than deleting the post. They could reveal who said it. I mean, if they *really* wanted to punish someone, a good public shaming would be the way."

"What!" My eyes about pop out of my head. "That would be a violation of everything VEIL stands for."

"Doesn't it stand for radical inclusion? Doesn't it stand for promoting art? Isn't its commitment to anonymity a way it hopes to erase systemic hate—exactly what this pinhead is promoting?"

"Listen—I'm not defending the post. I hate what it said. I'm just saying, if Burmkezerg personally went in and told the world who said it, he would be violating the principles that govern the entire community. It's a slippery slope."

Harold waves me off. "The slippery slope is a logical fallacy."

I throw my head back. "No more debate team cheat codes! Don't make me the bad guy!"

We've had tiffs like this before—especially when Speech and Debate season's in full swing—and it's usually easier to overlook how much better Harold is at arguing. But that's when we fight over whether the book or the movie is better, or whether semicolons should even exist. It's never about something this personal. Harold must sense that, because he backs off. An uneasy quiet falls between us, an awkward I can't stand. It forces me to think back to an entirely different kind of charged silence, in the igloo, a lifetime ago.

Harold drums his fingers on the steering wheel. "So why are we going to this art store, anyway?"

I sigh in relief. "There's this person who's been posting a painting a day to VEIL all summer. And they always use these unique brushes. So anyway, I think I figured out who this person is IRL—Jeanne Romanoff. And I overheard her saying the brushes got ruined and she can't afford to replace them."

Harold glances my way. "So you're going to buy her new brushes?"

"Yeah."

"Just to be nice. Because you've enjoyed her artwork."

"Yeah?"

"Are you going to give them to her personally?"

"No. I was thinking I could leave the brushes somewhere. Or sneak them into her bag or something."

"A surprise present," Harold says with a smile. "I should've guessed."

As a matter of fact, he *should* have guessed. Harold's been the recipient of about 85 percent of all surprise gifts I've given in my life.

There's something about surprise gifts that makes them better than birthday presents or goodies under a Christmas tree.

Like when my dad surprised my mom with tickets to a sloth habitat while we were on a UCSC-funded trip to Costa Rica. Not only is she obsessed with sloths, but it forced her to take a day off to enjoy the jungle paradise on a trip otherwise filled with research. A picture of Mom crying with joy while a sloth wraps its long, clawed hands around her finger is framed on our mantle and actually blocks their wedding photo. But I've always thought the sloth photo was a more accurate portrait of my parents' love for each other.

"So—just to sum up—you're going to spend money on fancy paintbrushes and give them to someone, without taking any credit, all because you appreciated the artwork they posted to an anonymous app all summer."

"That's about the gist of it, yeah."

Harold shakes his head.

"What?"

"Nothing—that's just . . ." He looks at me like he's recalling a fond memory, lips curled in the hint of a smile. "Of course you are. No one else would do something like this."

My heart skips in my chest. I duck my head to hide a smile. "I just hope it works."

"What was her name again?" Harold asks, pulling into the art store parking lot.

"Vivian Maier. I've been flipping through the art book Patton got me. Her stuff is amazing."

We pull up to the giant art store and I get the same feeling I had when I went to Toys "R" Us as a kid. I have the urge to throw my wallet at the cash register and grab as much stuff as I can carry.

"Uh-oh," Harold says. "I recognize that look. That's the same look I had on my face the first day of camp. They had literally every piece of lab equipment I'd ever heard of and a bunch of stuff I'd never seen. It was nuts."

"Aw," I say, nudging Harold. "You absolute dork."

"Thank you, thank you," he says. "But seriously, I can't spend too much time here. My parents kind of don't know I left the house? So we should make this quick."

"What?!" I stop in the middle of the calligraphy aisle. "Harold Johnson, you *lied* to your parents?"

Harold sighs, picking up and putting down inkpots. "There's just a lot of pressure from them right now," he says. "They got really excited when I came back ready to talk about college. Like, *really* excited. They made a new Gantt chart."

Gantt charts are terrifying spreadsheets that help people juggling, like, seven hundred different projects to keep things straight. The Johnsons have that Silicon Valley blend of idealism and exhaustive work ethic. It's what made them into a tech industry success story, but sometimes they misapply it to situations that call for a bit more chill. I'm sure they're eager to "disrupt" the college application process and get Harold accepted to every Ivy League school and Oxford besides. But it's taking a visible toll on my best friend. The fluorescent lights emphasize dark circles that have appeared under Harold's eyes. And he walks with a kind of stooped-shoulder lean, like he's carrying all those college application books on his shoulders.

"You're only a sophomore! They don't think that being in every single club at Belfry is pressure enough?"

Harold frowns. "There's a little more to it than that. They just want the best for me." Before I can chime in, Harold presses on. "Anyway. They think I'm just sitting in the car. In the garage."

"As usual," I say, joking.

Harold doesn't laugh. "Pretty much."

"You know, joining clubs—those aren't, like, contracts signed with blood," I say, passing row after row of canvases to lead us to the watercolor aisle. "You can always quit."

"Quit?" Harold scoffs. "Yeah right."

"Don't think of it as quitting. Think of it as . . . suspending involvement," I say. "Postponing engagement. Rain-checking responsibility."

We stroll past a wall of coloring books. One shelf is full of white paint-by-number globes. I give one a gentle spin, waiting for him to chime in with some romantical statement about the poles. Waiting for him to remember the igloo. But Harold is lost in thought.

At the end of the aisle, I pause, turning to look at him straight on. The slouch in his posture puts us eye-to-eye. The spark feeling is back, that new *something* that generates between us now, like he's flint and I'm kindling. This moment feels important, suddenly. Like right now, in this arts and crafts store, Harold has the chance to make a different sophomore year for himself. For us.

Harold steps in. My eyes flutter shut. I feel the warmth of his body as Harold reaches for my face and . . .

Past me, grabbing something in crinkly plastic just behind my head. I open my eyes and see he's holding up a pack of brushes.

There they are: the special nylon Korean brushes of Jeanne's dreams.

"Thanks."

"Is that what you wanted?" he asks. "I really should be getting back."

I stare up at him. His golden-brown eyes betray nothing. "Yeah," I say, clutching the brushes to my chest. "That's it."

Walking back to the car, I swing the bag holding the brushes between us.

"Have you posted to VEIL yet?" Harold asks, out of the blue.

Even I can hear the tinge of fear in my laugh. "Of course not."

A distant foghorn buzzes over the sand dunes lining the parking lot.

"It's okay to be involved in things, you know," Harold says. "To take risks. Stress isn't something to be avoided. It's the thing that makes us grow."

"Spoken like a true Johnson."

Harold's resigned sigh twists my heart. "Guilty."

CHAPTER 9

The brushes sit in my backpack, tied with a bright yellow bow. My heart beats a little faster all day thinking of the moment Jeanne will see them. I haven't had this rush since that afternoon in Harold's bedroom when he was packing for camp, waiting for the twinkle lights on the igloo to catch his eye.

But Jeanne and I don't have art together until fifth period, after lunch, which drags on forever and ever. I'm so desperate I even consider crashing Harold's Pismo Beach Disaster Relief Club meeting. Thankfully, on the way to the quad I notice a scrum of people scrambling for something: a stack of zines with a familiar hand-lettered title.

THE BELFRY BARNACLE

I gasp.

Yesssssss!

The *Barnacle* first appeared last year. The zine is a few photocopied pieces of paper folded and stapled at the seam to make a booklet. No one knows who created it, or whose words and collages fill its pages. But the little zine has had a far reach: The *Barnacle* runs a Page Six gossip-column feature filled with blind items that have crushed relationships, strained friendships, and inspired the official high school paper—the *Belfry Bulletin*—to launch an investigation into which cafeteria employee was putting silverfish in the Chinese noodle salad. Someone got fired and the entire *Bulletin* staff won a national student journalism award. And still, the tipster, whoever writes the *Barnacle*, remains at large.

At first, the whole school was certain it was someone who worked for the *Bulletin*. But the faculty advisor, Ms. Goo, swore on penalty of axing the entire journalism elective that nobody on her staff was responsible. By the end of last year, almost everyone at Belfry was convinced the *Barnacle* was a spiteful side project by Gaby Avila, who won her spot as president of student government by running a scorched-earth campaign. But Gaby graduated last year and went off to Dartmouth. Then about two weeks ago, someone started posting things to VEIL: a screenshot of the layout for the *Barnacle* in Photoshop, and a workspace covered in photocopied collages, an X-Acto knife, staplers, markers—all the makings of the zine the student body (and faculty) has come to love and fear in equal measure.

Whoever makes the *Barnacle* is still at Belfry, and even with the VEIL posts, we're no closer to identifying them. Tantalizing.

I grab a copy and duck out of the crush of people. Then I lean against the side of the library, adjacent to the sophomore benches. Far enough away not to be annoyed by their inane conversations, but close enough to make it seem like the exclusion was my choice.

This copy of the *Barnacle* looks like a banger:

The True Story Behind the Sudden Cove Bell Tower (and What Lives There Now)

and

Bye-Bye, Starbucks Parking Lot: Where This Year's Seniors Are Spending Saturday Nights

and

How We Wasted Our Summer Vacations

I flip immediately to the second-to-last page, the one always packed with unverified gossip that everyone at Belfry immediately accepts as gospel truth.

A certain junior hosted a genuine K-pop star at their house all summer for a student exchange program. Sources indicate they exchanged a lot more than cultural insights, if you know what we mean.

By sixth period I bet I'll have overheard enough to figure out the identity of the junior in question.

The next item nearly makes me choke on my Pocky stick:

The *Barnacle* humbly asks, who is worse: the flamed-out troll who went completely regressive all over VEIL, or whoever went crying to their parents—raising the ire of the administration?

I blink at the page. This is the first time that a *Barnacle* gossip tidbit has had the slightest to do with me, and I can't say it feels great. What does it mean that the administration is aware? What, if anything, can they do? This is the actual nightmare situation.

Oy.

By the time lunch winds down, I'm ready to redirect my attention to Operation Secret Gift. When the bell rings, I force myself to walk slowly to art. All this excitement will have been wasted if I'm caught slipping the brushes into Jeanne's bag. If I've learned one thing from years of surprising Harold, it's the critical importance of waiting for the right moment.

About half the class is already seated when I arrive, including Jeanne and Loretta. My target—Jeanne's backpack—is slouched on the ground between their stools. Ms. H greets me and I'm temporarily distracted by a row of glossy prints lined up along her desk. There's something unusual afoot.

Pacing myself, I head slowly to my seat, trying to see if I can somehow slip the brushes into Jeanne's bag on my way. As I near the art punk table, I prepare to leap into action. But just then my feet tangle up and I have to take a staggered step to regain balance. Jeanne and Loretta look up and see me gaping at them, goggle-eyed. They stifle laughter as my cheeks burn.

Mission notcomplished, I shuffle the rest of the way to my seat.

"Hi, crocodile," Nate greets me with a doofy grin. "Did you ever notice that? That the alligator and crocodile sayings are only for when you leave? What if you want to greet someone in a reptilian fashion?"

Truly, this is the most ridiculous thing I have ever heard. And it's just the distraction I needed. "Nathaniel," I say, shaking my head. "You know that is some Grade-A Illuminati nonsense you're talking."

"See?" he says with confidence. "I've got you thinking." He touches his third eye with his finger. "It's all connected."

I cover my face, but my shaking shoulders give away that I am overcome with giggles. "You know what?" I tell him when I regain composure. "You're right. It is your solemn duty to remedy this oversight and make things more comfortable for our lizard overlords."

Nate rolls his shoulders and turns to the front of the class, satisfied. "That's all I'm saying."

Ms. H stands and the room quiets. "On my desk are examples of street art from around the world. I'll call you up by tables, and everyone will pick a different piece to inspire their own work. Let's start with Megan and Jason."

I sit up straight. When it's Jeanne's turn to pick, that's my chance to sneak over and slip the paintbrushes in her backpack.

"I don't want you to replicate these paintings, mind you," Ms. H says while Megan and Jason stare at the prints on her desk. "Pick based on how the pieces make you feel. What they make you think about. Then create something based on that reaction, in the medium of your choice."

It's Loretta's and Jeanne's turn next. I scramble for the brushes, tucking them in my sleeve. Ms. H calls on the girls and I flick my decoy pencil in front of Nate, into the aisle.

"What the . . . ?" Nate looks from me to the pencil, confused. He gets up to retrieve it for me. Darn his gentlemanly instincts! I grab his arm and tug him backward.

"Sit still, Prince Charming," I mutter as he falls back onto the stool. I go after the stray pencil, within arm's reach of Jeanne's bag. I say a silent prayer of thanks for all the times I've had to tuck a tampon in my sleeve—sneaking the brushes into Jeanne's bag is a snap.

Package successfully delivered—and pencil recovered—I rush back to my seat before Loretta and Jeanne return. Pointedly ignoring Nate's narrowed eyes, I watch Jeanne lean over Loretta's print, discussing their choices. The brushes sit, unnoticed.

Nate leans into my field of vision. "Um, Ivy? It's our turn."

By the time we approach Ms. H's desk, about half the pictures are gone. I recognize some of the pieces—like a Banksy that went for a zillion dollars at Sotheby's. But most of the art is new to me.

"Don't think too hard about it," Ms. H cautions from behind the desk. "What grabs you right away?"

Nate reaches for a picture of a huge mural that spans the side of a brick warehouse. It shows a man crawling into his computer.

Outside the computer, in the real world, the man's hair is cut high and tight like a marine. He wears a shirt and tie. But the part that's through the computer is completely different: His hair curls and floats away from his head, defying gravity. He wears a headpiece of gigantic peacock feathers. The man's outstretched arm is covered in tattoos that echo the headpiece's iridescent blues and greens. He clutches a handful of fire dragon flowers.

It's an incredible piece, and I'm impressed Nate chose it. But what do *I* want?

There are two that stand out. The first is painted on the tall, thin side of a building in a busy city. It's constructed to look like a black-and-white mirror image of the street in front of it, but in the center of the painting stands a woman holding a camera. It's a little eerie, actually, how much it reminds me of the cover of the Vivian Maier book. I know immediately what I would want to do as my response piece. But the thought of posing in shopwindows and other mirrored surfaces around downtown Sudden Cove gives me a kind of queasy feeling. Shot after shot where I was in the center of the frame . . . That's exactly the kind of thing one of VEIL's photographers could do, in a cool and interesting way. They'd get the perfect angle, capture just the right expression, to make it transcend a selfie. I'm just not good enough to do that.

The other image that jumps out at me is a smaller piece drawn over a storm drain. In it, a map of the world is melting toward the sewer.

For better or worse, that one speaks to me, too.

I grab the second image. Nate and I saunter back to our seats. Jeanne has found the brushes.

She holds them to her chest, eyes wide and brimming with tears. And to my horror, Loretta nods and smiles and is quickly engulfed in a massive Jeanne hug. Jeanne mouths, "Thank you, thank you!" over and over as I sit, agape.

Not only did I miss the fireworks-and-birthday-cake moment of Jeanne discovering the brushes, Loretta *clowning* Kim just took credit for *my* random act of kindness!

Venus freaking flytrap!

"So what's the story with this painting?" Nate asks, sliding my picture across the table to get a closer look. "Um . . . Ivy?"

I snap my mouth shut and focus on Nate.

"What's wrong?" Following my gaze, he looks over his shoulder to Loretta and Jeanne.

"N-nothing." My blood boils, but how could I even begin to explain why I'm upset? "Totally fine."

"Sure . . ." Nate isn't convinced, but I think he's picking up on the you-don't-wanna-know vibe. "So, this painting?"

I glance back down to the world leaking down the drain. "Yes. It reminds me. Of someone."

Nate realizes that no more information is forthcoming. "Well, that's a good place to start."

"What about you?" I look over at his photo. "That's stunning. What made you choose it?"

"Oh, you know," Nate says, staring at the picture. His voice softens. "It reminds me. Of someone."

We sit quietly for the rest of class while Ms. H talks about why she chose street artists for this assignment (". . . their ethos of deconstructing art, including corporate logos and imagery we see so often that we don't typically think of it as art at all, in an effort to make us think about what we surround ourselves with every day . . .") and how she wants us to create a version of a street art gang by building a community of artists at Belfry.

Nate worries the corner of his print between thumb and forefinger while staring into space, lost in thought. I watch Jeanne clutch at the brand-new brushes, stroking the bright yellow bow. And Loretta looks extremely satisfied with herself.

I am very Kermit-flailing-arms.gif.

The flailingness continues through the rest of the day. When the final bell rings, I find myself stomping down the hall just to burn off steam. I can't stop seeing Loretta's smug grin as she accepted credit for my do-goodiness. I wander aimlessly—nowhere in particular to go, but unwilling to sit down or go home.

I keep an eye out for Harold. There's always a chance that the Native Plant Advocacy Consortium let out early. Though Harold and I have been known to shout, mock, cajole, and various other forms of rile each other up, he also knows just what to say to calm me down. My parents go right for the "You think your problems are so big? Talk to the Amazon rain forest" global-thinking route, which is both unhelpful *and* depressing. But Harold listens to my complaints, acknowledges the general suckiness of the situation, and either comes up with a brilliant solution I never would have thought of, or recommends just the right Goldblum movie. He's got a knack for that.

While craning my neck to see if Harold's hiding around the bend of the A wing, I ram head on into someone walking past. I sputter an apology, but a blur of something familiar cuts me short. It's Ajeet Banerjee, who I've known since kindergarten. My most vivid Ajeet memory is of the time he played the back half of a burro in a fifth-grade play about California's Spanish missions. He fainted under the stage lights and ripped the burro in half, much to the horror of the first graders in the front row.

What stands out today is his backpack. It's a low-slung JanSport with a few scattered pins . . . and a tortoiseshell pattern. My memory skips like a scratched record. Red flags and buzzing alarms flash in my brain: It's the chemo poster's bag on VEIL, one of the many little identifying clues I memorized over the summer.

Ajeet nods and keeps walking, adjusting the backpack as it hangs off one shoulder. His friends bounce alongside him, laughing.

Could it be true? Is Ajeet Banerjee—the kid whose tapioca pudding tutorial gave the entire class food poisoning! the kid who dressed as Waluigi every Halloween!—also the VEIL poster who regularly brought me to tears with perfectly composed shots of life as a walking preexisting condition?

If that's true, then not only is Ajeet Banerjee an incredible artist, but he has cancer.

Ajeet Banerjee *has cancer.*

And I can't say anything about it.

Revealing what I know about Ajeet would totally violate VEIL's rules of artistic anonymity. And also, like . . . Judge John Hodgman's basic norms of etiquette. But watching Ajeet and his friends saunter off, I feel a physical pull to follow them, to do something, to look him in the eye and say, "I see you." I want him to know that his work matters. To me.

But his friends may not even know. I've spent a lot of silent passing periods and lunches eavesdropping on BHS gossip, and there hasn't been a peep about anyone spending the summer getting pumped full of chemo cocktail.

My self-righteous anger at Loretta Kim has been wiped away. But what it's replaced with—this strange sense of yearning and sympathy and helplessness—isn't what I would call an improvement.

I shuffle toward the bike rack, mind whirling anew.

4:56 p.m.

HAROLD

I'm back!

> **IVY**
>
> From where?

HAROLD

I was touring Berkeley. That's why I wasn't at school Friday

> **IVY**
>
> You weren't at school Fri?????
>
> I hate that I didn't know that

HAROLD

😕

Sorry I haven't been around more. Let's fix it

5:06 p.m.

HAROLD

Elbow's Temple?

> **IVY**
>
> Ooh
>
> You know just the way to my heart

HAROLD

Gnomes are the way to every girl's heart.

IVY

You're a liar but you're my liar, Harold Johnson

HAROLD

10 tomorrow?

IVY

yessss

HAROLD

See you then!

CHAPTER 10

Elbow's Temple is on one of the wide, suburban streets in Sudden Cove's swankiest neighborhood, about a mile from the ocean. It's flanked on either side by faithfully restored Victorian homes with well-manicured lawns and gleaming Beemers in the driveways. The "temple" is a series of brick buildings scattered around a giant garden gone to seed: Towering palm trees line the property like crooked fence posts, aloe plants have flourished to the size of hedges, and former koi ponds are now muddy slicks sprouting bushy reeds. It looks for all the world like an abandoned lot that should be torn down, burned, and saged clean.

I rest Leibovitz against the nearest streetlamp. I'm a little early. Never cared about punctuality till now, when arriving early means scoring some time to scroll VEIL. My phone is out, purple screen blaring, in seconds.

VEIL has taken on a somewhat new feeling now that there's a couple things I'm looking for in particular. Those things being whether Jeanne resumes her painting-a-day schedule, and anything from Ajeet. (Not to mention the ever-present dread that the homophobic degenerate will resurface. Ugh.)

There's something from the mysterious creator of the *Barnacle*: a photo of an empty box from Copier Comrade, the DIY copy shop downtown. "First *Barnacle* of the year flew off the proverbial shelves," the note reads. "More SOON." It's hard to tell if the post is a promise or a threat, which seems on brand for the *Barnacle*.

Another post has a familiar backdrop: a bedroom with bright yellow wallpaper and a four-poster bed covered with a rainbow quilt. Center frame is a record player set up on a steamer trunk at the foot of the bed. The owner of this delightful room posts videos of the vinyl records playing, all cast recordings of various musicals. The record sleeves sit propped behind the player. This time it's *Kinky Boots*. There's something new in this post, though: In the corner of the frame, I can just make out a few of the clothes hanging in the partially opened closet (if I zoom way the heck in, which I definitely do). I'd recognize the Day-Glo pattern of those maxi dresses anywhere. I'll be hornswoggled— the musical theater obsessive is Jaz Clarke!

Filing that away, I scroll on. There's another from a familiar poster whose black-and-white photos broke my heart all summer. This one is of a home office. One half of the office is stuffed with books, the desk in its corner piled with magazines and awash in the glow of an opened laptop. The other half has been emptied, clear of everything but dust. All summer, this poster has documented something . . . either a divorce, or a death. Someone has gone absent, or feels absent. It twists my heart up.

No sign of anything from Jeanne, or any pictures featuring a telltale tortoiseshell backpack. But there is something new. A picture of a brick wall covered in ivy, the type whose leaves have light edges. The caption identifies the ivy as *Hedera canariensis*.

Hmm.

A honk almost startles me into the road. Harold waves from the Golf. The engine dies and Harold unfurls himself from the car. He's always been tall, but he's grown leaner since he left for camp, to the point where his long legs now look disproportionate. He still looks disheveled and unrested.

None of that changes how I react at the sight of him. My heart leaps. My pulse races. I smile reflexively. Harold Johnson, human electric shock.

I walk toward the entrance to Elbow's Temple. It's an arched wooden door set into the crenellated brick wall surrounding the property, with a bronze handle right in the center, like a hobbit house. A faded hand-painted sign on the door features a strange drawing: a feline eye staring out from the center of a triangle. Underneath that is written:

ELBOW'S TEMPLE
A REWARD FOR EVERY BUSHEL

And underneath that, in smaller handwriting, it clarifies:

FIVE GNOMES PER BUSHEL

"Hey," I say.

Harold leans against the door, rubbing his eyes. "Hay is for horses."

I kick his toe. "Have you ever thought about how we only use alligators or crocodiles for saying goodbye? Never for greetings?"

He perks up, but only to give me a very *what the hellfire?* look. "Huh?"

"Never mind." I nod at the hobbit door handle. "Ready?"

"Is it possible to be truly ready for Elbow's Temple?" He holds the door open for me, so I have to duck under his outstretched arm. I'm close enough to take in the familiar Harold smell: textbook pages and Old Spice. My chest constricts. I feel the kind of buzzing in my hands and toes that lingered long after I crawled out of the igloo.

The secret of Elbow's Temple is that, despite its wild appearance, every inch of the property is carefully tended by unseen hands. That becomes clear to those who walk the pathway made of stones, crushed seashells, and sea glass that twists and turns through the jungle-like interior.

Chip Elbow himself was a builder who made his fortune constructing half of Sudden Cove's opulent mansions in the gold rush days. Then—as the story goes—he lost a son in the Great War and holed the rest of his family up behind a great brick barrier. When World War II erupted, Elbow added new brick structures on the expansive lot. Bunkers? Emergency shelters? Additional houses for the multiple wives some claim he married in secret? No one really knows. At the same time, stained glass embedded with eerie shapes and occulty symbols was added to every building on the premises.

Chip Elbow had Some Stuff.

The last time Chip was seen by anyone outside the Elbow family was a winter night in the midst of World War II, when a particularly cruel storm crashed into Sudden Cove's harbor. Elbow braved the driving rain to affix a metal pole to the brick fence—a radio antenna. Elbow lay on a mattress he'd dragged onto the front yard, clutching headphones to his head and scream-ing into the storm that he could hear Germans sitting in their subs just off the coast.

Supposedly the property is still looked after by one Elbow or another. Some say Chip haunts the place. My hyperlogical mom and dad would cringe to hear me say it, but I think Chip still walks the grounds by night, ever watchful for the Germans and the storms they bring.

But all the stories are just window dressing for the real draw of Elbow's Temple: the gnomes.

Once inside, visitors pick a fork in the path and follow it. They'll begin noticing pops of unexpected color—bright red, blue, yellow, or orange cones protruding from palm leaves, or wedged in the crook of a juniper bush. Gnomes.

Visitors collect all the gnomes they find while they walk the garden paths. They all lead back to the Victorian manse's grand back steps. Not a sliver of the mansion's interior can be seen: The windows at the top of the steps are stained glass and musty old drapes are drawn within. A sign at the back steps reads "Rewards," and points to a metal door underneath the stairs. There's a chute, like a mailbox, where visitors can drop off their gnomes. Five to a bushel—no more, no less.

Another chute with a plastic cover, like the winning end of a vending machine, is inset in the door at ankle-height. After the gnomes are shoved in the chute (they clank and rumble for an alarmingly long time), you wait for the dispensary slot to give a metallic *clink*. Open the flap and: boom.

Reward.

I've gotten buttons, hand-painted beads, mood rings, fortunes freed from their cookies, erasers, googly eyes. I heard one time someone got a winning lottery ticket.

Shockingly few people visit Elbow's Temple, which suits Harold and me just fine. Anyone too creeped out by stories of grief-stricken men building temples to house what remains of their minds doesn't deserve a collection of plastic glow-in-the-dark hands, anyway.

"Which one?" Harold asks, eyes squinting against the sun.

We try to take a different path every time, and though we used to be here at least once a month, I swear we've never repeated a route.

"Mmmm . . . left," I declare, setting off with confidence. We fall into an easy pace, each scanning the garden like hunters after prey. A grim-faced gnome with a red hat and a corncob pipe peeks out from behind a bougainvillea bush. I climb in and grab it, trying not to crush flowers under my feet.

"I have something to tell you," Harold says after a minute of friendly quiet.

My heart flips. I carefully avoid eye contact and keep my voice at a reasonable volume. "Oh?"

"I thought a lot about what you said about VEIL. And about your random act of kindness. I realized some of my frustration is that I felt helpless, you know? VEIL is this thing we can't control, run by someone who doesn't answer to us."

Harold pauses when he spots something half-buried behind a riot of fuzzy cacti. Oh-so-carefully, he reaches in and unearths an upside-down gnome.

"The way I see it," Harold says, brushing dirt from the gnome's rosy cheeks, "VEIL means so much because it's a place where people can express themselves without being judged. And that's an admirable goal. But we should be able to feel free from judgment without giving up our identity, you know? I think it's a matter of creating better safe spaces among people we see all the time." He takes a breath. "So I've decided to start a club."

Oh.

My.

Blazes, that's the MOST Harold solution to a problem I've ever heard.

I look up at him with a confused smile. "Oh yeah?"

"Yeah. A Pride Club. That VEIL troll was taking aim at gay people at Belfry specifically, and when you think about it, it's terrible that an advocacy group doesn't already exist at BHS. The lack of support for that community might be part of the reason that idiot felt like they could say something so awful."

"Wow!" A grin stretches my cheeks. "That's incredible!"

"Thanks. Sasha Oh is going to be my co-founder. Did you know she came out as bi last year? It kind of went under the radar because she did it the same day Jared Beaver got taken out of Spanish AB in handcuffs for—" Harold stops short, focusing on something over my shoulder. Reaching up into a crawling vine, Harold digs out a sun-faded gnome who looks like he's been trapped there for ages. As we continue down the path, he adjusts his three gnomes under an arm. "I get why you love VEIL so much. But I don't think online communities can ever truly replace in-person activism. And . . ." Harold pauses. I brace myself as he goes on, "I was hoping this time, you might want to join. You know—show your support."

Something tells me Harold means support for more than just the LGBTQ+ community at Belfry. He's asked me to join a dozen clubs over the years, and I've always come up with some excuse. Harold can't accept the idea that I'm not really a *joiner.*

Of all the clubs he's put up, this one is the most compelling. But my mind immediately jumps to what this commitment would really look like: spending lunch under a classroom's fluorescent lights, eating grocery store cookies, and trying to make small talk while Harold chats easily with everyone. Inevitably, the other club members would wonder why someone as confident and well-adjusted as Harold bothers to spend time with me. Or, worst-case scenario—I get asked to come up with ideas and maybe even stand up and talk in front of the club, or the school. My skin crawls just imagining it.

And, though I voted for Brian Marantz for class treasurer last year (Brian's been openly gay ever since I can remember, and Lionel Steelhammer came out when they started dating in the spring), and I contributed to Renee Holmes's GoFundMe to pay for ASL classes so she could start a YouTube channel signing movies featuring queer characters, I haven't done much to support classmates who are out, or questioning. I want to be a good ally, but I'm not really close to . . . well, anyone but Harold. What if I started taking an active role now? Everyone in the club would think I was a faker, only there because of my best friend.

Harold's face falls at my hesitation. "Come on, Ivy. I know you care."

"Of course I do!" My voice squeaks. "Obviously I care. But joining a club . . ." I cringe and curl my arms up uncomfortably. "It just doesn't feel right. It isn't me."

"But you're such a sweet, generous, thoughtful person." Annoyance creeps into his voice. "I don't understand how you can feel so strongly about so many things and stay silent."

Silence isn't the same as inaction, I want to tell him. Just like wanting to be anonymous isn't the same as being scared to be yourself. But it's intimidating to contradict Harold; he always has the moral high ground. For him, it isn't worth believing in something if you aren't doing anything about it. Same for my parents; it's like none of them know how to set the bar lower than saving the world.

It felt like making a difference when I put those paintbrushes in Jeanne's bag. It would feel like making a difference if I found a way to make Ajeet smile. But I don't know how to explain that to people who think as globally as Harold or my parents without sounding lazy or uncaring.

"Aren't you worried about taking on one more thing?" I ask, avoiding the battle I can't win. "You're already sleeping in your car."

Harold narrows his eyes at me. "How did you know about that?"

"What?!" I nearly drop my gnomes. "I was joking. You're really *sleeping* there?"

Harold sighs. "Only once or twice. It's just so quiet."

"How do Angie and Stuart feel about a club interfering with your full-time job researching colleges?"

His expression hardens. "Starting this club is the most important thing. I can still make time to tour campuses. Somehow. And I might be able to take a step back from a couple other clubs if I have to."

Dang. Giving up other club commitments? He's super real-deal serious about this. I shake my head. Harold finds three more gnomes, but I spot only two more before our path dead-ends at the Victorian's back staircase. Silently, Harold hands his spare gnome out for me to take. I give him a shy smile of thanks and throw my bushel into the metal chute.

Clang.

The reward: a miniature Magic 8-Ball. While Harold tosses his gnomes into the chute, I give the 8-Ball a shake and ask the obvious question: Should I join the Pride Club?

It is unclear, the 8-Ball says.

"Thanks," I mutter, glowering at it. "What did you get?"

Harold straightens, holding his reward in his palm. It's a single tarot card: the Tower. It's on fire, with people falling out of it. Or maybe they jumped.

"Cheery," Harold says.

I don't know what we expected, but neither of us left Elbow's Temple with what we wanted.

CHAPTER 11

The first sign of trouble when I walk in the front door is that my parents are both staring, heads cocked at unnatural angles, at their phones. They squint at the screens like they're grading a particularly terrible term paper. As one, they look up at me over their reading glasses, frowning identically. My heart sinks. I know I'm in trouble, but I'm not sure why.

Dad quickly clears that up.

"So. What is VEIL?"

Both parents flip their phones around, showing me the purple feed. The color usually fills me with an expansive feeling of possibility. Now it feels like a secret that's been exposed. It's like I walked in on my parents reading my diary.

Tossing my backpack at the foot of the stairs, I sink into my favorite chair and sigh. "How did you hear about VEIL?"

"The school called."

That makes me sit straight up.

"They wanted to alert all the parents about their position on the recent homophobic incident that took place on VEIL," Mom says. "I said I'd never heard of it, and was told to 'speak honestly with my student about homophobia and the dangers of social media.'"

Ha. I have a pang of sympathy for the administrator who tried to tell my mother how to talk to her kid.

Mom continues: "I checked out the app. And it looked strangely familiar." She picks up a stack of pictures resting on the couch between her and dad. They're a few of the ones I took of my favorite posts.

"What the hell?" I blurt out.

Dad holds up a hand. "These pictures were scattered on the floor of your room. Some of them were in the hallway. Community space." He shrugs. "We were concerned."

I cross my arms.

Mom shows me her phone again. "So, what is this VEIL, exactly? What are you posting to it? Did you see this homophobic post? Do you know who wrote it?"

"Let's take these one at a time," Dad says. "Explain VEIL to us."

I pout. "You can download the app but can't bother to google it?"

Sass is the wrong choice. Both parents' expressions immediately darken to a look I call "Professor Face." There's no laugh lines or eye twinkles now. Only sternly furrowed foreheads and an implied threat of a failing grade. I cough and drop my eyes. "It's an app where people can post things anonymously."

"What do *you* post there?" Mom asks.

"Nothing."

Dad narrows his eyes. "You expect us to believe that?" He shakes one of my pictures in the air. "Your room is papered with dozens, hundreds of pictures you've taken. You never leave the house without a camera dangling from your neck. Why would you have the app and never post to it?"

I shrug.

"Why?" Mom echoes.

"I don't know . . ." I stare at my knees. This feels like a repeat of my fight with Harold, and I still can't scrounge together the words to explain why what feels right to me just . . . feels right. Does everyone have to justify their feelings this much, or is it just me? "I haven't wanted to."

Mom doesn't look like she believes me, but the interrogation moves on. "Fine. But just so we're clear, I want you to realize that nothing you put on the internet is truly anonymous. Ever. Got it?"

I nod, snippets of Burmkezerg interviews floating through my mind. But my sense of self-preservation tells me now isn't the time to contradict my parents with the word of an idealistic tech billionaire.

"This homophobic post," Dad says, taking over questioning again. "Was it as bad as the school made it seem?"

I think of all the posts that went up in response—all the poems, pictures, rumors at school, and finally even Harold deciding to stretch his schedule to the breaking point to do something in direct opposition to VEILgate. "Yeah," I admit. "It's bad."

They exchange a meaningful glance. "And no, I obviously have no idea who wrote it."

Dad raises an eyebrow. "What would you do if you did?"

Hmm. Tarring and feathering feels too close to the truth for me to throw it out there as a joke. "Well, for starters, I'd never talk to them again. And I'd report it to VEIL."

"Not to the school?" Mom asks. "Not to us?"

"You want me to tell you every time someone says something terrible on the internet?"

That does the trick: Both Mom and Dad crack a smile.

Dad nods. "Well, you've got us there."

Mom shakes her head. "This is like freshman orientation all over again."

"Okay." Dad perches at the edge of the couch. "Now we get to the part where you ask *us* questions. And we tell you what we're planning to do."

Alarm bells ring in the back of my mind. "Um. I guess I'll start with: What are you planning to do?"

"Well, the school is holding a special PTA meeting to discuss their approach to action," Mom says. "And we got a call from another parent who is considering filing a lawsuit to get VEIL to reveal the identity of the person who posted it so they can be dealt with appropriately."

"What?! They can't do that—the app is anonymous. That's the whole point!"

Dad interjects. "Ivy, that post was hate speech. That might

be debatable as a First Amendment right, but it definitely doesn't abide by the Belfry High code of conduct."

"How did Belfry even get involved in this? It all happened on an app—VEIL people are dealing with it in their own way."

"VEIL's method of dealing with it is *not* dealing with it, at all. The company isn't going to do anything unless something forces its hand." Mom's taking on her Professor Voice and I don't care for it. At all.

"You don't understand," I say. "VEIL is all about freedom of expression. If they told everyone who posted that, what's to keep them from revealing who posted every single thing on the site?"

"Would that be so bad?" Mom asks. "From what I can tell, most of what's posted there is benign. Some of it's quite good, actually. Why don't people want to be associated with their work?"

I drop my head into my hands, thoughts racing too fast to wrangle into coherent sentences. People like Mom and Dad and Harold can't relate to the fear that what they create might be taken the wrong way, misunderstood, or worst of all, ignored. Who's going to hate on a scientific study, or protest the formation of an altruistic student group? They don't understand what it means to create something that represents a weird, maybe even ugly, part of yourself, and then put it into the world. What if everyone hates it? Or worse, what if no one else relates to it, and you get confirmation that you're the only one who feels that way? Staying anonymous is like getting permission to do the scariest thing. But if VEIL revealed the identity of a user—even one—those reassurances wouldn't mean as much anymore.

"That just isn't the point!" is all I can come up with on the spot.

"Why don't you help us understand?" Dad asks.

Have you ever wondered what it would be like to have a psychotherapist as a parent? Well, it cannot possibly be worse than professor parents who are coached by psychotherapists every school year on "How to Relate to the Youth." It leads to these circular conversations where I feel like I say everything I have to say, and more, but I never get more correct.

"What if I didn't tell you about this app because I didn't want you to have to understand?"

Mom sets her phone down on the table. "Okay. I think we've said enough on this for now. Thank you for answering our questions, Ivy. We'll talk more about it after the PTA meeting this week."

I seize the chance to cut and run, grabbing my bag and taking the steps two at a time. Crappily, the piles of photos spread across the floor of my room remind me that even this place isn't entirely safe. I sweep the prints up and pull a plastic storage tub out from under my bed. I label and date every sleeve of prints, line them up in the tub, then snap the lid into place and shove it back under the bed. If my parents get the urge to pry again, I bet digging around in a hidden container with a closed lid would make them feel more guilty than picking pictures up off the floor.

Door shut, pictures put away, and music set to ear-bleeding levels, I throw myself on the bed.

As awful as the VEIL troll's post was to begin with, it's been compounded times a million by opening my online community up to attack from all sides. Harold and my parents and the PTA think they're doing the right thing, trying to help people. But it feels like I had access to a super-special tree house and now people I love are sawing down the tree—all the while telling me it's for my own good. What makes them think that attacking VEIL is the same thing as protecting the people who love it?

I'm *pissed*.

It's like they can't see the hypocrisy in judging something they've barely bothered to understand.

I think of all the pictures I just tucked away. Dozens and dozens of them are of VEIL posts that brought a smile to my face, or tears to my eyes. *That's* the good that VEIL can do. And, thinking of Jeanne's face when she was hugging Loretta to thank her for the brushes, I realize that that's also the good VEIL can do.

Through me.

It's not exactly playing by Burmkezerg's rules to figure out who VEIL posters are, but it doesn't come close to publicly revealing user identities. It's based on clues they themselves made public—and I'm not telling the whole wide world. Just using what I know for good.

While the haters pick up pitchforks and come after VEIL, I can make its users feel better. Feel appreciated. Feel like someone *gets it*.

And, luckily, there's an obvious place to start: with Ajeet Banerjee.

CHAPTER 12

G AY!
A ll it takes to make
Y ou know you're not welcome.

G rievance, or silent majority?
A nyone's guess. It just makes
Y ou realize it may never feel safe to say

G ay
A s a way of saying
Y ourself.

I read and reread the poem, eyes brimming with tears. When Mom opens the driver's side door I wipe my face discreetly and pull myself together. The last thing I want to have to do is explain why I look bleary-eyed, especially because of something on VEIL. The app is beyond taboo with the parents now.

Plus, Mom is driving me to the Bigfoot Museum to meet up with Nate. Gift horse's mouth and all that.

Nate and I were paired to do an art project together last week. Well, actually what happened was Ms. H told us to partner up and Nate turned right to me and started talking about ideas. He just assumed we were going to pair up. That made me so happy I felt dizzy for hours. And the assignment is pretty rad, too. "Much of the time, art is how we communicate meaning when words won't do the trick," Ms. H said. "Get into pairs and prepare a presentation on the iconography of a concept, or an abstract idea." Nate hesitated for maybe half a breath before saying: "Bigfoot."

He is full of surprises.

Mom connects her phone to the car stereo and turns to me with a guilty look. "Do you mind?"

She loves to listen to recordings of other professors' lectures while driving. Mom's big on multitasking. Usually I find it to be the most befuddling and annoying thing on earth—like, take a day off, you know? But today I welcome the distraction.

"Sure."

Mom drives while a nasal male voice drones on about the popularization of native landscaping. I stare out the window and *feel*. I'm upset that the artists on VEIL are still upset. I'm a confusing mix of frustrated and sad that Mom and Dad are getting involved in the PTA for the first time, to fight one of my favorite things. I feel guilty for not agreeing to join the Pride Club. And I'm nervous about seeing Nate outside of school. What if he gets wise to the fact that he is *way* too cool to be hanging out with me? On the other hand, how will I keep my cool with Nate Gehrig for more than sixty minutes at a time?

A deeper part of me feels a nostalgic kind of sad. Sitting in the passenger seat while sunlight filters through the evergreens lining the mountain road, I think: I should be sitting in Harold's car. He and I should be going to the Bigfoot Museum together. He loves museums dedicated to concepts or oddities. When he read about the Museum of Broken Relationships in L.A., he pasted it to the news wall and was super serious about driving down to go see it. But that was before camp.

Of course.

Finally, the feelings get to be too much. I need a distraction. I tilt my phone to hide the screen from Mom and scroll through VEIL. Jeanne is back on the daily painting kick—today's is of a new pair of cat-eye sunglasses. Not many other new posts, but one stands out: a picture of a wrought-iron fence being slowly swallowed by ivy. The text of the post is just "*Hedera helix.*"

Hmm. Two ivy posts in as many weeks . . . Three would officially make it a trend.

The Bigfoot Museum is in an old wooden house on the road that wends around the Sudden Cove Redwood Forest Reserve. There's a giant wooden sign above the front porch that reads: "Bigfoot Museum!" A life-sized hand-carved statue of

Bigfoot and a Bigfoot baby stand beside the entrance. Next to the Bigfeet, looking like a mismatched member of the family, is Nate.

When he looks up, there's a half a second where his face glows. His hazel eyes crinkle at the corners and his grin is so big you can count all his teeth.

"Who is that?" Mom asks when Nate waves.

"No one." I open the door and step outside.

"Wait—what?" Mom's voice rises an octave.

"Nothing, ever. I'll call if I need a ride home. Bye!" I shut the door and skip to Nate's side.

The car window whirs down and Mom sticks her head out.

I give her a look that says, BE COOL.

Mom pauses, then just says, "Have fun!" before driving off.

Nate looks at me with a knowing smirk. I hate that smirk. I love that smirk. "Getting dropped off by your mom, huh?"

I roll my eyes and adjust the bag hanging off my shoulder. "Yeah, yeah."

He nudges me gently with his elbow. "I would've picked you up, you know. I forget that you're only a sophomore."

Blushing, I stare down at his Jordans. Okay, so. Here I am, at the Bigfoot Museum. On a weekend, midday date with Nate Gehrig.

Wait.

Is it a date?

How often do dates involve school credit?

He holds the door open and I walk under his arm, which gives me flashbacks to Elbow's Temple with Harold. Nate smells like cedar and campfire. And an electric thrill courses just under the skin as I duck past him, knowing his eyes are on me. It's shades of the igloo *moment*, which makes me feel guilty. Like Harold might be somewhere, witnessing . . . whatever this is. I feel like I owe him something. *I don't*, I remind myself, thinking of the moment I walked into Harold's room when he got back from camp and was greeted with a frown rather than a hug.

We stand in the entryway of the museum and stare around the cramped space. Beside the unoccupied front desk is a penny press. The old machine has a coin slot and a lever to the side. Pulling the lever smooshes the penny, leaving it flat and impressed with the image of the cryptozoological wonder traipsing through the woods. *THE BIGFOOT MUSEUM*, it reads in arched letters across the top. Then, underneath: *BE A BELIEVER*.

A leather-bound visitor log sits open on the desk. The most recent entry, from someone named John Green, reads: "Keep up the good work."

The entryway opens to a hallway lined with glass display cases. They're filled to bursting with paraphernalia: artifacts and newspaper clippings of Bigfoot sightings. Nate tells me about a survival expert's ten-part podcast series about his encounters with the elusive Sasquatch.

"I thought you'd never been here?" I ask.

"I haven't," he says. "Always wanted to. I asked my parents every year for a while to have my birthday party here. Which . . ." He looks around. "I get now why they wouldn't want to do that."

"Why didn't you ever just come here, on a non-birthday?"

Nate pauses. He taps a finger on the glass of the display case. "My family isn't really into stuff like this."

"Stuff like . . . ?"

"They're pretty literal. It can be hard to present them with new information," he says after a minute. "They see things as pretty black and white." His gaze drifts, lost in thought.

I step away to give him space and examine a series of plaster replicas of footprints that a Saskatchewan farmer claims to have discovered on his property.

Nate moves past me into the next room, which is all about countering the haters who think Bigfoot is a hoax. We're surrounded by blurry photos that truthers all over the world have taken. A long, waist-height display case packed with maps, compasses, field journals, and various other items from amateur Sasquatch hunters lines one wall.

"Hello." A man who looks like an old-timey sea captain smiles at us from behind the counter. He looks like he should be smoking from a pipe and telling kids ghost stories. "Welcome," the man says in a raspy voice. "If I had to guess, I'd say I have a couple skeptics on my hands."

I tilt my head, considering. "Agnostic."

The man nods approvingly. "And you?" he asks Nate.

Nate folds his arms. "Listening."

The man grins. "Well then. Let me tell you my story. I've lived in the woods of Northern California all my life. And my first memory—honest to god, my very first one—was seeing Bigfoot."

I lean my elbows on the counter, chin on my hands.

"I was four years old," the man says. He's obviously told this story before—like maybe hundreds of times. "I was camping with my parents near a stream. At some point I was washing my hands in the water, alone, and when I looked up—there it was." He stretched his arms to reach as high as possible. "It was this tall," the man says. On the wall behind him, at the tips of his fingers, there's a line of red duct tape and a sign that reads, "IT WAS THIS TALL."

"A huge, hairy beast. It looked at me, right in my eyes. I can still see it—clear as day. The most vivid memory of my life." The man's eyes go distant, like he's staring off into a dream. "My dad called after me. Bigfoot waded out of the stream to the other shore and disappeared into the woods.

"Now, I know what you're thinking: I was young. I can't possibly be remembering this right. And it's true that some more recent sightings have been debunked. But"—the man grabs an encyclopedia-sized research book and starts flipping through chapters filled with pictures of cave drawings, etchings, and blurry photographs—"tell me why Bigfoot, or a large, hairy humanoid matching its description, has been recorded by almost every human society for more than thirty-five thousand years? We know that half a million years ago, Neanderthals and *Homo sapiens* first genetically diverged. We also know that for hundreds of years, the two shared enough genetic similarities to interbreed. And even today, there are still vast swaths of land that have never been fully explored, and remain primal. Untouched by human interference."

Nate's arms are uncrossed now. He leans against the counter, too, eyes darting from the man to the book.

"I'm just saying," the man continues, "it's more difficult to *disprove*. Life, and this planet, still holds mysteries for us. What if, instead of holding so tightly to the odds that this story isn't true, we let ourselves be open to the small chance that it is?"

He shuts the book, turning to place it back on the shelf behind him. Nate and I exchange a wide-eyed look. My heart races.

The man faces us again. "And let us not forget the possibility that Bigfoot is a multidimensional time traveler."

I blink.

Nate stands back up. "There it is."

We listen politely as the man gives us a hard sell on time travel. At the first opportunity, Nate jumps in to ask about the signs that promise a "Once-in-a-Lifetime Photo Op!"

The old man directs us to a self-guided tour in the museum's back garden and we politely excuse ourselves.

Another life-sized Sasquatch statute holds laminated pamphlets for the tour. A short stone path winds through the backyard.

In the center is a huge fountain with a Bigfoot figure, midstride, carved pterodactyls perched on its head and shoulders. Burbling streams of water stream from their open, screeching beaks.

"I'm starting to think you misled me," I tell Nate as we head down the path. "I think you're a believer."

I'm just teasing, but Nate looks around, considering. Plaques placed along the carefully manicured path describe the ancient plants. "Like I said, my parents are pretty literal," Nate says. "I grew up thinking things either were, or they weren't."

I nod but stay quiet. It seems like Nate has more to say.

"The older I get, the more I learn about the spaces in between. Right and wrong, real and not real. It's like those lizard people you were talking about."

"The Illuminati?"

"Yeah—I mean, isn't the world more interesting because stuff like that is out there? It almost doesn't matter if there are really lizard people running the planet. I like that we can talk about it, and live in 'maybe' instead of just 'yes' or 'no.'"

I want to tell him that a lot of people would think it mattered deeply if an elite group of lizards wearing human suits were actually running the world. But I think he's being metaphorical. And interrupting would be rude.

Nate shrugs. "Like that guy said. The world still holds mysteries. And that feels . . . hopeful." He motions to the garden. "And in this case, hope looks like a jumbo-sized nightmare creature covered in hair, who might be able to hop dimensions, and/or travel through time."

The path doubles back toward the house. The fountain gurgles, and a crisp fall breeze sighs through the redwoods and oak trees swaying overhead.

Nate adds, "If everyone could talk about it like this, I think we'd discover things about people we wouldn't quite expect."

"That everyone's a weirdo?"

"Maybe. I think there's so much about each other that we don't know. Even if we're close to someone. People keep secrets, or are afraid to admit things."

Past a massive palm tree, we stumble on the fourth wall of this backyard sanctuary: the side of the garage. It's covered in a full landscape mural, rolling hills blanketed with evergreens and a distant volcano belching ominous smoke. Standing in front of the mural is a life-sized cutout of Sasquatch with a hole where his face should be.

This must be the Once-in-a-Lifetime Photo Opportunity.

"Well," Nate says. "This is . . ."

"Amazing?"

"Yup. Got your camera?"

I'm way ahead of him. I take pictures of Nate posing with, behind, in front of, and alongside the Bigfoot cutout, statue, and fountain.

But my favorites are when we go around front. The sun

dances at the tops of the trees, and the afternoon light slants sideways on the Bigfoot Museum sign. I get shots from every possible angle, playing with shifts in the rapidly dying sun. Nate models beside the carved Bigfoot and child, the shadowy light washing out everything but his outline.

I try not to think of all the times Harold patiently indulged me like this. All the hours he stood where I asked, posing as I demanded, so I could learn the basics of photo composition. Even a few weeks ago, the idea that Hunky Nate Gehrig would be doing the same would have been enough to unmoor me from reality. But today it feels . . . well, kind of normal.

"You're a great model." I hide my blush behind the camera.

"Anything for a friend," he says.

Oof. Friend.

A few minutes later, we pull into my driveway. Both my parents' cars are here, so I want to get into the house before raising too much suspicion. That, and I need to be out of the company of Nate Gehrig to process all my thoughts about being in the company of Nate Gehrig.

"This was so fun," he says. "Let's talk more on Monday about the project, okay?"

"Yes. School. The project." Normal friend things to discuss. How perfectly normal and friendly. "Sure thing."

I get out of the car and am about to shut the door when Nate calls my name. I lean in.

Nate looks up at me warmly, his expression strangely relieved. "I just want to say . . . Thanks. For making my little-kid birthday dreams come true."

I smile and toss my head, loopy with joy. Immediately I feel like an idiot. And yet! Nate thinks I'm great! I make his dreams come true! "You're welcome," I say, with as much normalcy as I can muster. "See you Monday."

The door slams, Nate's car kicks into reverse, and he's off, leaving me with a fifteen-dollar plush Sasquatch souvenir, two rolls of film to develop, and a whole lifetime's worth of questions.

CHAPTER 13

Later that night, I flip through my photos of Ajeet's VEIL posts. With my sketchpad and a stub of charcoal, I try replicating the most gut-punchy shots, drawing loose shapes, seeing what feels right. The post I choose to draw is a mirror selfie. In it, Ajeet wears a shapeless hospital gown and stands beside a thin metal pole, holding a bag of medical liquid, its drip tube twisting out of frame. The background is a blur of floral arrangements, balloons, and stuffed animals—the brightly colored ephemera that fills the temporary homes, and lives, of the sick. In the foreground, blocking the bottom of the mirror, is a black plastic garbage can brimming with half-eaten Jell-O cups. The optimism of well-wishes fades far behind the tasteless reality of being chronically ill.

The image popped into my mind every so often over the summer, reminding me of the hidden lives of everyone around me. It seems like the perfect picture to thank someone for sharing a secret.

I stay up late watching *Cats & Dogs* and *Run Ronnie Run!* as a feel-good double feature while I pencil out the drawing.

Sunday I mix colors to *Igby Goes Down*, outline and paint to *Dallas 362*, and shade to *Spinning Boris*. On Monday morning I gently roll the painting and tie it with more yellow ribbon.

It's only underneath the library eaves at lunch that I realize: In the midst of my inspiration explosion, I completely forgot my actual assignment for art class. The photo I picked from Ms. H's desk—the world swirling down the drain—is still sitting on my desk, untouched.

I spaced. Fully, galactically spaced.

Now, I'm not exactly a model student. But this is different. This is the assignment Ms. H was going to use to determine which of us were artists and which were casual hacks. Skipping it entirely could make Ms. H feel like she was wrong to think I had something special. She might even question Patton's judge of character. Why get excited about someone who can't even get it together enough to turn in the very first homework assignment?

I wrestle with whether to turn in the painting of Ajeet. It's strong work and I know it. But submitting work based on other people's art is ethically questionable at the best of times. It feels needlessly risky now, when the whole school is so focused on VEIL and what's being posted there. If anyone recognized the source material for my painting, I could get in big trouble. Plus, I'd be outed as someone who spends their time and talent re-creating other people's work. Again, not exactly a ringing endorsement of my character or work ethic.

Needless to say, the rest of my tuna sandwich goes uneaten.

I rehearse a tearful apology as I shuffle to the D wing. Holding my breath, I turn the corner—and stop in my tracks.

Ms. H stands in the hall, surrounded by everyone from art class. She spots me. "Ivy! Great. Everyone's here. Follow me!"

I try to keep up with Ms. H as she power-walks down the hall toward the quad.

"What's up?" I ask.

"Do you have your camera?" Ms. H looks at me with laser focus. I nod. "Great," she says, looking ahead of her just in time to avoid running into Zoltar, the mechanical fortune-teller the junior class set up as a fund-raiser for homecoming. (The theme is the movie *Big*, but apparently all life-sized keyboards in the Bay Area have been semi-permanently leased to tech companies for their game rooms. That leaves us with creepy carnival automatons. Yay.) Zoltar waves at us, cackling mystically, as we pass.

"Why?" I ask.

"You'll see." Ms. H zips past me.

"Hey," a deep voice says in my ear. I nearly leap out of my shoes. Nate laughs like scaring me is the funniest thing he's ever done.

"Been a while, crocodile," I tell him, smoothing my hair.

Nate nods approvingly. "It has. In the last forty-eight hours, have your feelings about Bigfoot changed?"

"Nah." I fall into step as we follow the rest of the class. "Still thoroughly friend zone."

It's so easy to joke with Nate. But I find myself glancing around, wary that Harold will be wandering campus and see Nate and me laughing and smiling at each other.

I have to shake my head and remind myself: It doesn't matter what Harold sees. He's made his feelings (or lack thereof) very clear.

We take a shortcut through the cafeteria to the Z wing. The Z wing centers around a three-story geodesic dome, which houses the Belfry musical theater program. Two smaller domes flank the larger one, and the rest of the wing is made up of faded temporaries and storage buildings.

The BHS musical theater program was never supposed to exist. During the '50s space race, the dome was built as an observatory. Some locals who worked at Stanford and the Jet Propulsion Lab donated equipment. But when the Cold War took an ominous turn, some paranoid Sudden Covers freaked that having a mini lab in their backyard might make them a target for Soviet ire. So they ripped out the telescopes, donated the large equipment, and transformed the dome into a theater space.

Ms. H approaches one of the smaller domes. It's still at least two stories high—taller than the rest of the sprawling, ranch-style school. I always assumed it stored old theater equipment, or janitorial accoutrements, or the bodies of principals past. Ms. H holds up a key and waggles her eyebrow, a slightly crazed look in her eyes.

She opens the door to the dome and disappears. From within, she shouts: "Come on!"

I lean into the doorway, squinting to adjust to the dim light. The trick of domes is they feel so wonderfully large inside, like you've shrunk to fit inside a genie's lamp. I squint to follow the smooth curve of the wooden beams up to where they meet in a starburst of structural integrity. A couple skylights keep the dome from deep-space darkness. Even a foot or so from the door, I feel stuffy; uncirculated air settles on my skin like a layer of dust.

Nate ducks in after me, and has to crouch down far longer before he can stand without brushing his perfect hair against the ceiling.

Ms. H is in the center of the cracked concrete floor, spinning, smile a mile wide. "What do you think?"

"I thought there was stage equipment in here," I say.

"So did Principal Hermann. There's been high turnover in the janitorial department, so somehow this place got overlooked. Until the building code instructor came by, and then"—Ms. H waves her hands like she's presenting a game show prize—"this little baby became allllllll mine."

I raise the Canon to capture Ms. H's over-the-top joy. I frame her in the bottom middle of the shot, dome arcing over her head in a halo of mid-century architecture.

"It's amazing," says Jeanne. "But what do you mean, all yours?"

"It took an extensive PowerPoint and a lot of groveling, but I was able to convince Principal Hermann to give this space to the art department—meaning me. And I'm going to turn it into Belfry High's first ever student-run art studio and gallery space."

Nate raises his hand. "What's that mean?"

"I'm glad you asked!" Ms. H shuffles to the far end of the room. "I was thinking we could put a potter's wheel here. And here"—she spins clockwise—"a dozen or more easels. And we can throw up freestanding walls to create a kind of museum space, with rotating exhibits."

She returns to the center, hands clasped. "No matter what we do with this space, I want it to house student art. Starting with some of you. The pieces you submit in this class will be gathered into a portfolio that will grow over the semester. At the end you'll all get to present a body of work. The top five will get the chance to show at the gallery opening."

I try to imagine the dome as Ms. H does, with freestanding walls and a fresh coat of paint. And my photographs hanging on the wall.

I want to make that daydream a reality. The urge hits me unexpectedly hard. My brain whirs a million miles a minute. I've always been passionate, but this is something different—this is competition. If I'm not chosen to show my work, I will pack a bindle with croutons and ride the rails for the rest of my life.

I *really* want this.

Too bad I whiffed on completing the *very first* art class assignment.

Nate leans sideways to whisper, "You've got this in the bag."

I wince. The dome acoustics make everyone else hear him, too. Loretta turns, ever so slightly, eyes narrowed. We aren't the only ones exchanging cutthroat looks.

Art class just got interesting.

Ms. H claps. "Your new assignment, with a partner or alone, is to come up with a way to use the space. Go crazy. Imagine what we can do in here, and bring in blueprints or a diorama or an edited image, whatever."

Nate bumps my arm with his. "Partners?"

I wouldn't have trouble coming up with something on my own for this space. But . . .

"Aw, c'mon," Nate says. "You might not need me, but I definitely need you."

I smile up at him. "Sure."

"Oh BLEEP," Ms. H says, causing the room to lapse into silence. (She didn't really say "bleep.") "The assignment!"

My stomach drops.

"Ugh. I forgot to collect it from every class. You know what? Who am I kidding? I'm not gonna have time to grade it for a while, with all this going on. I'll give you an extension, deadline TBD."

I nearly float to the top of the dome, I'm so relieved.

Nate and I sit and discuss dome potential. Turning it into a giant hedge maze; putting a boxing ring in the center; making the entire thing one giant nude body-painting studio. I'm laughing so hard that I hope my grin, and the dim lighting, mask the insane blush in my cheeks.

Ms. H walks over. "Can I borrow you a sec, Ivy?"

"Sure." I follow her, my stomach dive-bombing. Even though she gave us an extension, the irrational part of my brain is convinced she *knows* I didn't complete the assignment on time. I'm donezo.

Ms. H leads me to a door set into the far side of the dome. She wrestles it from its jamb, exposing a long closet space.

Ms. H breathes a sigh of relief. "Oh good, they're all dead," she mutters.

"What?"

"What? Nothing." She steps into the closet, pushing the door all the way open. Once again she holds her arms out, presenting the room as one of the seven wonders of the world. "I thought this might make a good darkroom."

I blink at her, my mouth wide open in shock. The little closet space is cramped, poorly lit, and smells like stale saltines. But . . . with a small table to hold the developing station, and the corner crisscrossed with twine and clothespins to make a drying station, and a red light dangling from the ceiling like in the movies . . .

"We'd have to seal the doorjamb," I say absently, walking the space.

"Easy." Ms. H leans against the door, arms crossed. She smiles.

"A few metal shelves against the far wall to hold the developing liquid and extra paper . . ." I nod to myself, turning around and inspecting every corner. "This could work. It could totally work."

"I can't afford to help you with any of the supplies," she says. "But if you want to take on this project, I'll save the closet for you."

"Yes," I say without hesitation. "Yes, please."

Ms. H books it when the bell rings, ushering us out of the dome. She has to do the reveal all over again with her next class. As she hustles through the cafeteria doors, my heart floats like a freshly filled balloon.

"What was that about?" Nate asks.

"She thinks there might be space in there to build a darkroom," I say. "She asked if I wanted to build it."

We start walking toward the cafeteria. "Build the darkroom yourself?" he asks. "Do you know how to do that?"

"No," I say with caution. "But I know someone who does."

The minute Ms. H made her wild-'n'-crazy proposal for what to do with the closet, I immediately jumped on one thing: how much Harold Johnson is going to wig out with wanting to help me with this project.

I practically skip through the cafeteria, imagining sitting through Harold's explanation, in gruesome detail, of exactly what the chemicals are doing at every step of the development process. Inevitably, he'll draw molecular structures on scrap paper and get into the history of whoever created the periodic table of the elements. He'll start tapping his long fingers together and get that special glint in his eyes that appears when he's caught up in something wildly dorky, every gear in his brain spinning. That adorable dimple beside his lips when he's concentrating.

It'll be just like old times.

A new studio. A reprieve on my first forgotten assignment. The chance to spend more time with Harold . . . I've been touched by an angel.

And I haven't even gotten to the best part of my day yet: giving Ajeet his present.

My plan was to give it to him anonymously. This week I confirmed the location of his locker, and though it hurt to think of folding the painting, I was going to flatten it and slip it through the vents. Then I'd loiter nearby and wait for that pure moment, when he realized it was a gift made especially for him.

But I'm so hyped up right now. Plus! Recalling Loretta's smug grin when she took credit for my gift to Jeanne fills me with fresh, hot rage. Surprise gifts aren't all about me. I get that.

But that doesn't mean I'm gonna be ~super chill~ about some-one else getting all the credit.

And there's a few more minutes left in passing period . . .

I grab my backpack straps and jog through the cafeteria, waving at Zoltar as I jog past. His cackling sets the pace as I rush to Ajeet's locker.

CHAPTER 14

Ajeet and his friends are gathered by his locker. If there's one thing more intimidating than a group of guys standing around together, laughing loudly, it's a group of *tall* guys standing around together, laughing loudly.

But I ride the wave of adrenaline right to Ajeet's side, silencing his friends mid-guffaw.

"Um, hi," I say.

Ajeet looks at me, bewildered. "Hi?"

Trying to avoid the scrutinizing stares of his friends, I lean in. "Can I talk to you? Alone?"

He looks pained. "The bell's about to ring?"

His friends start to back away. One of them, a guy named Seth with a military buzz cut, mutters, "Come on, man."

I shift my weight, not sure what to say to convince him—especially without blowing his cover. The thing about secret-keepers is they are far more likely to pick up on subtle cues. Ajeet's dark eyes examine my face, then clear with some kind of understanding. Over his shoulder, he tells his friends, "I'll catch you after."

They give him a *your funeral* look and lope off.

"What's up?" he asks.

Setting my backpack down, I take out the painting and hold it out. The yellow ribbon has frayed a bit at the ends.

He looks at my offering like it might be poisonous. "What is this?"

I roll my eyes. "Just . . ." I flap my hands. "You know. Jeez."

Ajeet holds the painting like a scroll, its edges curling over his fingers. Gone is the furrowed wrinkle of suspicion that had lined his forehead. He's gazing at the picture, eyes wide, jaw slack. "This is . . . How did you . . . You painted this?" He turns the painting to me. "How do you know about this?"

I shrug. "You put it on the internet."

"Not with my name attached."

I point at his backpack. "Not exactly inconspicuous."

Ajeet sighs. "I knew I should have gone camo."

He can't look away from the painting. I can't stop smiling as he examines it, eyes growing misty. "I—um. I couldn't stop thinking about that picture. When VEIL reset, I felt like it had been stolen or something." I take a breath. "I just couldn't let it go."

Ajeet presses his lips together. He lowers his eyes and releases a shaky breath. "It was a hard summer."

I look to the ground and give him a moment to collect himself. To be honest, I need one myself. Gifts are a vulnerable act. In the moment of giving, we express the depth of our feeling. But

134

there's always the chance that a gift missed the mark, or that the person receiving it just doesn't feel the same way. When Ajeet's fingers grip the painting tighter, and he takes a few uneven inhalations, I feel proud, and happy, and a strange sort of heartbroken all at the same time.

The bell rings. We're both late.

"I guess I just wanted you to have it," I say gently.

Ajeet rolls the painting up with care. He takes me in, head to toe, all the suspicion he'd regarded me with when I first rolled up now gone. "I'm not telling people," he says, cautious.

I mime zipping my lips.

Ajeet nods. Then, without warning, he steps into my space and gives me a tight hug. He smells nice, like nacho cheese and aftershave.

"Thanks," he says, taking a step back. "Just—thanks." Then he heads down the hall, holding the painting to his chest.

He loved it, and I'm glad. But Ajeet has no idea what his reaction means to me. He's the first person besides Harold and my parents to really see the kind of artwork that matters to me.

I'm so glad I didn't hang back in the shadows for this one. Because *that* is what a random act of kindness is supposed to feel like.

CHAPTER 15

After my encounter with Ajeet, I float through sixth period and fly from school to Aperture Rapture, my heart rate never settling all the way back to normal. I throw the door to the shop open, welcoming the clatter of bells.

I've interrupted Patton while taking a selfie with an old Kodak Instamatic. He stands quickly, composing himself. "Ivy!" he says, tugging his beanie down. "Was hoping you'd come in today."

"Slow one?"

"Oh, you know. The usual." Patton heads back behind the counter. He slides an envelope of prints across the counter to me. "Great batch this time. Though, I have to say, it's starting to feel like I'm developing someone else's work more often than yours."

Oof. That puts a significant dent in my swell of fine feeling. I grab the envelope and shove it in my bag. "It's been hard to find time to go shooting."

"I get it. How's Candace?"

It takes me a beat. "Oh, you mean Ms. H?"

He grins. "Yes. It's weird to think that Candace is a teacher. We went to undergrad together—go Banana Slugs. How's she doing?"

"Great," I say, thinking of her spinning joyfully in a dome just a few hours before. "Super great."

"Well, isn't that just super great?" Patton winks. He rings me up but, when I turn to go, calls me back. "Hey—Ivy." He pauses, dropping the silliness he plays up when I'm around. "I'm serious about the pictures," he says. "Using your energy to document other people's creativity is a bad habit. It can start to feel like the only way, if you let it."

What can I do but nod?

Deflated, I let myself out.

The light outside is fading into dusk. The setting sun turns the thin clouds Creamsicle orange and rose-petal pink. This kind of light creates the most gorgeous silhouettes, where shadows become subjects in their own right. I shuffle over to a bench.

Peeling back the Aperture Rapture envelope's tacky adhesive seal, I take out the most recent batch of pictures.

The past couple weeks have been particularly rich on VEIL. Anger and hurt from the troll have inspired searing ironic commentary, heartfelt empathy, and raw pain. One poster began a new gardening project, planting row after row of flowers that will bloom into a living rainbow flag. Another started labeling random, boring stuff (their plate at Panda Express, the aisle of hand soap at Safeway) as "gay." (Postscript: "If you look hard enough, everything is gay! #Blessed") And another hand-sewed dozens of patches with grinning rainbows that say "SO GAY!" with the promise to hand them out to all their friends at Belfry.

Flipping through the pictures I took—post after post of encouragement, resistance, self-reflection, honesty—reminds me that every last one of these VEIL users is just like Ajeet. They all have private struggles and secret pain. I have to believe they would all be moved if they knew how much their work meant to people like me.

That's why I take pictures of their posts. And, though I don't know what Patton would say to that, I realize it doesn't matter. *I* don't think it's a waste of film. The opposite, actually. And the thrill of surprising Ajeet today has only made me more sure that finding all the VEIL users I can is how I want to make a difference.

I tuck the prints back in the envelope and scroll through VEIL. (It's been at least an hour.)

Just a couple swipes in and an image makes me gasp. It's a shot of my bike—right where it's parked now, in front of Beach Reads. The user has gone filter crazy and the bike looks super badass with the sunset in the background. In the caption, the user wrote, *How freaking amazing is this bike? Wish I was ridin in such styyyyyyle.*

I peer around the parking lot, alert for any movement. Whoever took this picture did so in the last fifteen minutes—they

could still be nearby! My scan of the lot ends at the Beach Reads'
fluorescent-lit front door.

Jumping to my feet, I walk slowly past the bookstore window, staring into the brightly lit space. Sure enough, sitting
behind the counter, scrolling on her phone, is Jaz Clarke.

"Gotcha," I whisper.

The random acts of kindness have only just begun.

To: msianmalcolm@geemail.com
From: tha_burm@veil.yolo
Subject: Important Message for Our Sudden Cove Users

Dear VEIL user,

Hey there. If you're getting this message, it's because you live in the Sudden Cove, California, area and you may be impacted by a decision we at VEIL have been forced to make.

As you may be aware, on September 26, a member of the VEIL community put up a text post that many found to be offensive. Here at VEIL, we take reports of offensive content very seriously. But as users know, we take our commitment to anonymity, privacy, and the right to freedom of speech seriously as well. Our customer satisfaction and legal departments have been working hand in hand on this issue to weigh our options, always thinking first of what would best serve our users.

However, while we conducted a thorough internal debate, outside forces were at work. VEIL has been confronted with several legal actions from users, parents or guardians of underage users, and institutions like local high schools.

Our main concern has been the protection of our users. Anonymity is embedded into every part of the VEIL user experience, and we know that many of you would not be using VEIL without that steadfast commitment to privacy. However, the pending legal actions have given us much to think about where it concerns our younger users.

Though VEIL's core tenet is the freedom of expression, the idea that any of our younger users would be distressed or caused emotional or psychological damage due to something they read, saw, watched, or witnessed on our platform is unacceptable.

In an effort to work with the affected community—your community—the VEIL team has decided to cooperate with the users, parents, and institutions who seek to address the root causes of harmful speech in their own ways.

I wanted to write this letter personally to explain our reasoning. And I want to take this chance to reiterate VEIL's commitment to the privacy of its users. This represents an extraordinary circumstance, and we hope that the preventative measures that VEIL and this community take together can keep similar incidents from happening in the future.

I hope you can understand, and that you will join us in recommitting to making the VEIL community an open and welcoming place, for all users, for many years to come.

One love,

Rake Burmkezerg and the VEIL team

4:47 p.m.

HAROLD

I'm guessing you saw the email from Burmkezerg?

IVY

Yes

ugh

what does this even mean?

"cooperate"

HAROLD

It means they told the PTA and Belfry who posted the homophobic stuff

4:55 p.m.

IVY

?????

Well???

WHO WAS IT

5:01 p.m.

IVY

HAROLD

HAROLD

Sorry!!! Sudden rush at the voting registration booth

We're at the boardwalk today and it's been amazing.

Signed like 20 people up to vote! 😊😎

HAROLD

Ok, ok, yes

It was Tag Gehrig.

IVY

. . .

wut

like, Nate's brother?

HAROLD

Yeah. IDK if he's getting suspended or cut from the football

team or what but

It was definitely him. Sasha told me

IVY

Wow.

5:11 p.m.

HAROLD

You ok?

IVY

Yeah, I just

Gotta process this.

5:16 p.m.
HAROLD

I think you need a little Goldblum.

IVY

I think you're right. 😊

HAROLD

CHAPTER 16

Belfry is alight with gossip. I spend all day eavesdropping on talk of VEIL's dramatic reveal that Tag Gehrig is the homophobic troll.

". . . kicking him off the team entirely? No one is gonna go to Saturday's game . . ."

". . . probably just transfer, at this point. Nate'll probably go, too . . ."

". . . second period, Nate looked like a freaking zombie . . ."

My heart is breaking for that freaking zombie. Though I don't know everything about Nate Gehrig, I am confident he does not share his brother's opinion. I can't imagine him ever even *thinking* "gay" as a slur. And I've never had a sibling, much less a twin, so I don't know what it would feel like to be asked to answer for someone else's mistakes.

While I tilt my head toward every hushed conversation, I also remember what Nate told me at the Bigfoot Museum, about his family being so closed off. Way, way more. I wonder if Tag was just repeating something that he hears at home. But who knows? There are infinite reasons why people say or do ignorant, hateful, or just plain mean things. It doesn't excuse them.

I don't have Nate's entire schedule memorized, but I do know the location of his fourth-period class: economics with Gillis in K-8.

Begging out of class early, I sneak over to the K wing and wait.

Nate's the last person to exit. He ducks his head, feet shuffling half-heartedly. When Nate spots me, his whole body shifts. His shoulders drop, his eyes widen, and he beelines right at me for a hug. I wish that I could grow three sizes so Nate could feel as warm and safe and protected in my arms as I feel in his right now. Instead I just squeeze him around the middle as tight as I can.

Nate holds on to me for a long time, until the hallway is almost empty. When he steps back, he turns his head to the side for a moment, wiping his face with his hands.

"So. Good day so far?" I say weakly.

Nate breathes out a relieved sigh and half a laugh. "A breeze."

We stand near each other, letting all the crappy stuff around us settle for a minute. I'd been spinning my wheels trying to think of what to say to Nate, what I can do. The next move is suddenly very clear. "Hey." I grab his arm. "Let's get out of here."

Nate raises an eyebrow. "Like—skip?" He looks around, as if he's waiting for a reason to stay. It doesn't arrive. "Why the hell not?"

Why not indeed.

We walk toward the parking lot. There are so many questions I want to ask, but I'm not sure what's okay to talk about. There's so much I don't know. How does Nate really feel about his brother? Does he get caught up in this guilt by association all the time? And the worst thing—what if he doesn't disagree?

Nate clears that up quickly.

"My brother is an idiot," he says as we weave through cars.

"That's one word for it."

His shoulders sag again. "Yeah."

Nate stops at his car, a hunter-green Ford Focus, and unlocks the doors. The car has scuffs and scrapes, and the back seat is bursting with cleats, shoulder pads, practice jerseys, orange cones, and other football ephemera. He clears a duffel bag off the passenger seat to make room for me.

When I settle in, he puts the key in the ignition but doesn't turn it. "So, you're on VEIL." It isn't a question.

I nod.

He sighs, looking blankly through the windshield. There's a nervous energy in the car. I can't quite get comfortable in the seat—it's well-worn to fit the body of a gigantic dude. The car has the damp musk of guy sweat, which doesn't smell entirely bad.

"What do you post on the site? Would I remember your stuff?"

Hesitating, I stare down at my knees. "No. I don't post."

That doesn't seem to be the right answer. Nate takes a breath, biting back whatever he was about to say.

"What about you?" I ask. Nate grimaces, fingers tensing around the key. "You don't have to tell me," I add, hurriedly.

Nate turns the engine over. "Where do you want to go?"

"I don't know, but we can't get caught." The thought of Mom and Dad getting that phone call makes me squirm. I've spoiled them by being such an introvert; at this point, if I so much as jaywalked, they'd freak.

"Copy." Nate eases out of the parking spot. We crane our necks for the lot attendant. Coast clear, Nate floors it. We peel onto the two-lane road leading past Belfry and under the highway, ocean-bound.

For a while, we drive in silence. I roll down the window, letting in the cool tang of salt air.

Nate rubs his eyes, then flips the blinker on. "I could go for some coffee."

"Late night?"

He nods. "Kind of."

We park in front of Vacuum Coffee on the five-block stretch of Sudden Cove that serves as a downtown. Sudden Cove is big enough to have a pretentious pour-over coffee shop, but small enough that you can almost always find street parking right in front. Nate gets a fancy espresso drink. Like Harold, he has expensive taste. Harold has explained what a "flat white" is to me like seventeen times but I can never remember.

I get a mocha with extra whipped cream. The drink of the proletariat.

Vacuum Coffee is on the traffic roundabout at the center of town. The most important streets branch off from here, like the spokes of a wheel: Pike Street for shopping, Ocean Avenue for tourists, and Melrose Boulevard for townies actually looking to get home. Right off the roundabout is Vacuum, the Sudden Cove courthouse, the library, and an old Victorian-turned-law office. The middle of the roundabout itself is a park named after the only Sudden Cove resident to die in World War I: Tyler Flynn Memorial Park.

Nate and I take our overpriced drinks to the park and grab a cement table. The black-and-white checkerboard embedded in the tabletop is confused by random bird droppings.

Breathing a sigh of relief—or is it resignation?—Nate sets the drink down and rests his chin on his knuckles. "So, ask."

I cup the mocha between my hands. "How did you find out?"

"Everyone I've ever met was ready to text me about it," Nate says, eyes dark with anger. "And the school called my parents, obviously. Interrupted dinner to let us know: indefinite suspension, and permanently kicked off the football team."

"Do you think it's fair?"

Nate sits with that for a minute. He stares past me, at the row of empty swings swaying in the breeze. "My brother is an idiot. He needs something to show him how serious this is. But . . ." Nate shakes his head. "Tag also loves football more than anyone I know. He was sort of counting on it to get into college. This messes with his dreams about the rest of his life."

Wow. I try to imagine Harold being cut from every club, or me being banned for life from Aperture Rapture. We would be lost. Distraught. Then again, neither of us would ever do anything to harm another person on purpose.

"My parents were mad," Nate goes on. "But also confused? They didn't know about VEIL. We spent the first hour explaining it to them, and then we got this whole lecture about social media and temptation." He sighs. "Totally beside the point. And they never even asked if I was on the site—I just got the lecture right along with him. Bogged down in his crap. Like always.

"Tag has this personality that's so big, it kind of overwhelms everyone around him—usually me. At some point my parents stopped bothering to differentiate between us. Sometimes it feels like they don't know anything about me."

My mind flashes on my parents, who never thought to ask about art camp, or even community college classes for photography. Who've only framed pictures of mine when they're in them. Who only bothered to look at my art when they thought an app might be corrupting my mind.

He finally looks me in the eye. "My parents are mad, but not for the right reasons. They want to fight the suspension and the lawsuit. They won't listen to me, that it would be better to go along with it. To think about the people Tag hurt."

Nate closes his eyes, face settling into a frown. His thick chestnut curls shiver in the wind. I want to press the thin lines around his mouth, smooth them out. "They think they know everything," he says after a minute. "But so does VEIL. So does the school. What are we supposed to do when the people in charge are just as dumb as everyone else?"

I hesitate, then decide to go ahead and say what I want to say. "Well, I'm glad that *you* see that what Tag said was terrible. It sucks that you're all wrapped up in his consequences. That isn't fair."

That earns me a smile. A sad one, but I'll take it.

"Thanks," he tells me. "Thank you for getting me out of there. If I had to deal with one more person giving me the side-eye, I swear . . ." Nate's hands form fists. He releases them and, to my shock, reaches out to take my hands in his. My fingers are flush with warmth from the mocha. His hands are so much bigger than mine, so much colder. His fingers easily wrap around my wrists. My arms erupt in goose bumps.

I've grown somewhat accustomed to the intensity of Nate's hazel eyes, now that we see each other almost every day. But I don't think I could ever get used to this kind of direct eye contact, where I can count his lashes, and see how his eyes are darker around the pupils. My breath catches.

"I'm so happy I met you this year."

"Me too," I say, grinning.

Just as suddenly as his hands took mine, they fall away. "Hey." Nate looks over my shoulder. "Isn't that Loretta?"

I spin on the bench. A small group of people are gathered on the marble steps of the courthouse, a plain brown-bricked building with fancy Grecian columns to snazz up the front. Some of the people wear wrinkled suits and clutch briefcases: lawyers. Loretta stands between two adults who are dressed more casually. They look upset. I recognize the tall, stately blond woman to Loretta's right as Ainsley Condotta, her mother, who started AstralJuice and is the biggest name in green drinks this side of the Sierra Nevadas. The other person—wearing a brown leather jacket and rocking a thick mustache—must be her dad. The two hover around Loretta, every tic broadcasting the awkward sadness of the moment. There's a brief conversation and her parents share a stilted handshake. The discomfort is palpable; I'm actually cringing.

Loretta's dad gives her a giant hug. When they part, Loretta looks after him, wiping her eyes. Finally her mom calls after her. Loretta pauses. Grabbing her phone from her back pocket, Loretta kneels to snap pictures of the courthouse's steps.

"Lore!" Ainsley shouts impatiently.

Without a word, Loretta follows, phone clutched tight in her hand.

"Art class must be pretty empty," Nate says.

I refocus on him, and our picnic table, and the lukewarm remains of my mocha. I wonder if this was what Ms. H meant by "something to art about."

CHAPTER 17

Nate drove us down to the train tracks by the Boardwalk, where we walked along the mossy bridge, talking about our favorite movies, where Nate is thinking about going to college (somewhere in Southern California, so it can feel like out of state but be in-state cheap), and whether or not Mr. Ducca, the musical theater teacher, was dating Mr. Gillis, who taught econ (their subjects are too different to merit all the time they seem to spend together during zero period).

When the light began to fade, Nate insisted on going back to Belfry to pick up Leibovitz and drive me home. I had him drop me off a few blocks from my house, to avoid any potential questions.

Walking in the front door, I nearly crash into Dad. He and Mom are throwing on their coats.

"Oh, hey, hon," Dad says. "Off photoshooting?"

"Yeah," I say. That's a good enough excuse. "Where are you going?"

"To Belfry, actually," Mom says, adjusting the Banana Slugs tote draped over her shoulder.

"Huh? Why?" I stand in the way of the door.

"There's another meeting tonight, with the PTA and the administration," Dad says. The way he adjusts to face me directly makes me nervous. "It's about the VEIL thing. The Gehrig family wants to fight his suspension. They hired a lawyer. We're going to talk about what we want to do."

"Hired a lawyer to do what?"

Mom and Dad share a look. "The Gehrigs want to sue the school," Mom says. "And VEIL."

"The school has a lawyer, too," Dad adds. "Some of the parents *are* lawyers. Everyone wants to avoid a lawsuit. But we have to talk about options."

I drop my bag by the entryway table. "I don't understand."

"Tag's parents are upset that VEIL revealed his identity." Mom slips into Lecture Voice and my fingers curl. "And there are some parents who think that VEIL lacks adequate safeguards for underage users. They think a lawsuit might be the only thing to make VEIL change its rules."

"What? Change what rules?"

"Well, for one thing, VEIL should know which of its users are under eighteen. And they might consider blocking those users from seeing or posting some content."

"So the First Amendment is good and censorship is bad, except if you're a kid?" I flail my hands around my head, shutting my eyes. So many thoughts fly around in my mind, making it hard to put them in an order my parents will understand.

Dad tilts his head. "That's being a bit simplistic, Ivy, don't you think?"

"No, I *don't* think!" I snap. "You don't understand VEIL. Not at all. You can't imagine why someone would want to post things without revealing who they are? You can't see how what Tag posted *proves* that we need a space for that?"

"You said you aren't even posting to the site," Dad says gently. "I don't understand why you're getting so upset."

His tone, like I'm a misguided student in his class, is the last straw. "Because I don't know the people on VEIL, but they'd have more respect for my work than anyone I know in real life. And maybe the people on VEIL are only that inspired, or creative, or brave because they don't have to worry about mixing art with real life."

"Are you saying you don't think we respect your work?" Mom looks stunned.

"You never ask to see my photos. Until you dig through them without permission. You never talked about sending me to art camp, or setting up a darkroom."

Mom and Dad stand there, frozen.

I wipe angry tears from my face. "Whatever." I shove past Mom to the stairs. "Have fun at your meeting."

I slam the bedroom door behind me, throw my bag on the ground, and lean against the door. Tears leak from my eyes. The anger ebbs away, but I'm shaking all over. I feel empty, hollowed out. I've never talked to my parents like that. There's no way to know how they'll respond.

Downstairs, the door shuts, firmly.

So I guess that's how they respond. They leave.

The house phone rings. It's such an unusual occurrence it shakes me out of my anger-fueled fugue. I love the vintage house phone installed next to my door—it's light pink and has a curly wire and everything. It's perfect and, most of the time, silent. I take the phone from its cradle and tuck the receiver beside my ear.

"Hello?"

There's a fuzzy quiet, then a robotic voice kicks in. "Hello. This is *Belfry High School* calling to inform you that your student, *Ivy Harrison*, had at least one unexcused absence today. If you have any questions, please call the administration office between the hours of *7:00 a.m.* and *5:00 p.m.* each weekday. Thank you."

Well, I guess there's one benefit to my parents' litigious preoccupation: Without that message, they won't know that I skipped with Nate today.

Nate. He never gave me a straight answer about whether or not he's posting to VEIL. Which makes me think he *is* posting, and doesn't want anyone to know. Thus proving the point I was trying to make to my parents! I wish I could tell them about Nate and explain the other side of all this rigmarole about Tag. How it's hurting people the more and more they push.

That makes me think of Loretta, and Ajeet. And that's just the tip of the iceberg. The poster tracking their recovery from a terrible bike accident; the one on a quest to slow down time through any means possible; the one who posts overhead pictures of the dinner table every day—table always set for five, and only four plates clear at the end of the meal.

How can anyone not understand the beauty of this thing?

It's too much for me to handle.

That night, I go through my new bedtime ritual: playing ambient music while I get ready for bed; doing my twelve-step Korean skin care regimen by candlelight; redoing the hospital corners on my bed so I get that awesome cocoon feeling when I crawl under the sheets. And then, with my earplugs in and my face mask shoved up on my forehead, I scroll VEIL until I feel sleepy. Sure, that part means I'm flirting with insomnia. But late nights on VEIL are when some of the really good stuff goes up.

When I've nestled myself in freshly washed sheets and let the icy purple of the phone screen wash over my face, I see it: a photo of soaring Grecian columns.

One column slices the frame in half. Midday light casts shadows on each smooth groove. The light and composition creates an M. C. Escher effect of black-and-white shapes in mind-bending patterns. It's Loretta's picture from the courthouse. And the editing makes it clear just exactly who Loretta Kim is on VEIL—the poster who I figured was documenting a death or a divorce all summer. The one who posted the picture of the half-cleared office, and a two-car garage with one spot empty but for the outline of a vehicle that once sat there, dripping oil. The heartbreak was clear in every frame. Turns out it was Loretta Kim's heart breaking this whole time. And now I know why.

The random acts of kindness started as a way to say thank you. Now it feels like maybe I can say something else, something more, with them, too: like *I see you*. Like *your pain matters*. And maybe also a little of *parents just don't understand*.

I put the phone facedown on my side table. But sleep evades me for minutes, maybe hours, as my mind spins with plans.

CHAPTER 18

A bad feeling comes over me the minute I get to campus. Everyone's reading a new edition of the *Barnacle*. In blaring, sixty-eight-point font, the paper's headline reads:

ALT THE RIGHT STUFF:
TAG GEHRIG IS VEIL TROLL

Oof. I'm dragging a rolling suitcase crammed with development chemicals, plastic tubs, and a bunch of other darkroom stuff, so I can't enter the scrum for a new edition. I grab a copy out of the trash and get to first period early to dig in.

The *Barnacle* pulls no punches. Whoever's behind Belfry High's alternative news source is really, really pissed at Tag. They've collected unattributed quotes from Belfrians calling Tag things like "craven caveman," and "dud stud." (The *Barnacle* writer may be taking some leeway with the cleverness of Belfry students, but hey. Style's not a crime.)

Other highlights of the zine include praise for Mr. Ducca for opening the *1776* casting call to all genders for all roles: "Exactly the kind of thing Belfry needs right now, what with backward-thinking bozos like Tag Gehrig roaming the halls."

I turn to the last page of the issue, usually a grab bag of random artwork, or a crossword puzzle, or a reprint of the Sudden Cove police scanner transcripts.

This back page, however, feels the furthest thing from random.

"Guess which Belfry sophomore spent the summer in the chemo ward, but can now celebrate the joy of remission? No secret (anymore): It's Ajeet Banerjee and he's here to tell his story."

I nearly choke on my own tongue. Ajeet's op-ed is really an inspirational personal essay. It details in beautifully spare prose how he felt the day he was diagnosed ("on April Fool's Day because: the universe"), the people he met during the long hours he sat in a chemotherapy chair down at Kaiser, and how he's still processing the word "remission."

When I look up I realize the bell rang ages ago. Every single person in Ms. Matson's first-period chem class is reading Ajeet's essay—including Ms. Matson, who folds a copy of the *Barnacle* on her desk and discreetly wipes away tears.

I've barely taken my seat in second period when the office assistant appears out of nowhere with a note instructing me to head to the Z wing.

Dang! Harold is *good*.

I wasted no time in telling Harold about the darkroom project after Ms. H sprung it on me. Within minutes Harold asked for the room measurements and started a MetaFilter thread soliciting tips on DIY darkrooming. Obscenely early the following day, he sent me a Word doc with a list of supplies, infrastructure needs, and the game plan for today. Step one: Pull strings with his connection at the admin office to get us both out of second period. That way, Harold could spend an hour building the darkroom without missing any extracurricular commitments. (Who needs American lit or zoology, anyway?)

I roll my bag through the cafeteria. Harold waits on the other side. "Hello, darkroom hero!"

Harold bows. "At your service."

When we enter the art dome, two dozen pairs of eyes focus on us at once. Harold is unfazed, of course. From her perch atop an exercise ball, Ms. H waves us in. The dome has been transforming, slowly, into Ms. H's art studio vision. A freestanding wall splits much of the room in two, and a handful of easels are propped in a corner. Sawdust, paint sample cans, and random tools lie around the space.

I show Harold to the closet. Once inside, I unzip the suitcase and start laying out the materials:

1) An enlarger, an optical apparatus similar to a slide projector that projects the image of a negative onto photo paper. Patton helped me find a gently used one on eBay for hella cheap.

2) Photographic paper (matte > glossy).

3) Photographic developer and liquid for a "stop bath" that halts development.

    a. Also plastic tubs for the developer and stop bath.

4) Photographic fixer, which stabilizes the photo, meaning exposure to light won't mess with the image anymore.

    a. Also a plastic tub for the fixer.

5) Water for the final tub.

    a. Also the final tub.

6) Nails, twine, clothespins, and all the other stuff I want to use to let the prints dry.

For the record, all this equipment is Not Cheap. I initially shrugged off Ms. H's insistence that she could not afford to help me set up the darkroom. But after doing more research, it was clear that paying for chemicals and photo paper was on the expensive side. Luckily my parents rarely bat an eye if I ask for money for educational purposes. And now I'm considering it backpay for lack of art camp.

Harold sets up the cheap IKEA tables I got off Craigslist while I set out the chemicals and the tubs. I do what I usually do when we haven't seen each other in a few days: ask how things are going, then sit back and let the waves of club/student government/ SAT prep class drama wash over me. All these extracurriculars mean Harold's college applications will be impressive AF, but the true benefit is his access to every bit of gossip.

I'm cruising along in my nodding or oohing and aahing at the appropriate moments when Harold throws me a real curveball.

"So, I watched the documentary about Vivian Maier."

Huh?

"Huh?"

Harold raises an eyebrow at me, the incredulous *didn't you know?!* look I've been dealing with since fourth grade. "Yeah! It's called *Finding Vivian Maier*, and it's on Netflix. Duh."

"Dang!"

"You really should take one day off from the Goldblumathon and give it a watch," Harold says.

"I totally will." I set up the tubs in a neat row.

Harold pauses. "When you told me about her, you made it seem like she was kind of an inspiration for you."

Now it's my turn to narrow my eyes. "Yes?"

Harold shrugs. "Nothing. Well, I mean—just that you should watch the documentary."

"Harold!" I hate when he does this. It's so very *my parents* to be all, "You should find this out for yourself." He knows that bugs the hell out of me. "Just tell me!"

"Well—do you know why she was an unknown artist?"

I tilt my head. "Because she was all about the art. Wanting it to speak for itself, you know? Not wanting her persona to get in the way of the actual photographs."

The look on Harold's face is tragic. Like he just smelled the inside of a Tauntaun after I told him he'd have to sleep there to survive the night. "Uh . . . That isn't exactly it."

"What is it?"

Harold shrugs.

"Don't do that," I say, curt. "You know something and you've brought it up, so now you have to tell me."

Harold sets down the jug of chemicals he'd been holding. "She was antisocial. And kind of mean." His face contorts slightly. "The documentary interviewed kids she nannied and they said she was physical with them. Like, hit them."

I drop an entire stack of photo paper. "What?!"

"Yeah. She was pretty awful, actually."

I've spent hours poring over Vivian's photographs in the book Patton sold me. She had such an impeccable eye—decades before street photography was the lifeblood of style blogs and Style section editorials, Vivian was capturing the lives of workaday Chicagoans with grace and beauty.

Harold looks uncomfortable. "Listen, I'm sorry. I don't mean to be a downer. I know you love her work."

"Yeah. I do." With a sigh, I start picking up the papers. I pause, brushing hair out of my face. "You know, it feels like you're trying to make me feel bad for admiring her. It's just about the art."

Harold's turn to sigh. "That's the thing. I worry that you look up to Vivian as some brilliant artist whose anonymity was

164

an act of artistic purity—that isn't the case. She was a jerk and, like, maybe kind of a sociopath?" He shakes his head. "I don't know. Anyway. There are lots of normal, decent people who put their name to their work and survive criticism. It isn't actually life-threatening."

Anger floods through me. When faced with Harold, or my parents—people who prize being *logical* and even-keeled above all else—I find it almost impossible to express my rage. They don't take anger seriously, even if it's justified. Which I happen to think it is, right now, when my best friend is going out of his way to hate on one of my creative icons. I feel hot, and upset, and very unevenly keeled.

"You know what? Cork it, Harold. You don't know what you're talking about." He jerks around in surprise, his eyes wide. I stand up, forgetting the papers. "It must be satisfying to sit up there on your high horse, where you're saving the world all the time. Bet from there it's real easy to see what I should do."

"That isn't what I'm saying. Or doing." Harold shoves non-existent glasses up his nose, a nervous tic contacts can't fix. "And you'd know that if you bothered to come to a single club meeting. For any of them. Ever."

"What the heck? I am your best friend. I support everything you do. And I shouldn't have to go to a club meeting to prove that."

"Well, it would help!" He screws the lid on the jug of fixer and slams it on the table. "You're making me feel bad for joining these clubs and doing all this work for college. I'm trying to figure out my future. You act like I'm leaving you behind, when really you're choosing to stay back."

"Not everyone wants to go to an Ivy League college!"

"Well, *not everyone* might be able to get into an Ivy League college, if *not everyone* had any interest in trying!"

I stomp my foot. Seriously. Unironically. Childishly. "Lay off, Harold! I thought you were here to do me a solid."

Harold clenches his fist. "I am! Again! Like I always do! And yet you never show up for me."

Shaking my head, I point out the closet door. "Dude. Leave. I can do this myself."

He pauses for a moment. A thousand unspoken sentiments fizzle between us. Harold rubs his still-cropped hair, frustrated. Wordlessly, he marches out.

Ms. H and the rest of her class stare in our direction. "Oh, take a picture," I sneer. Heather Schusterman raises her phone and snaps one.

"It's an expression, Heather!" I slam the closet door, shutting myself into darkness. Sinking to the floor, I sit with my back against the door, head in hands. Now I'll go from being the aloof Goth kid who doesn't talk to anyone to being the *angry* Goth kid who yells at the future homecoming king. Cool cool cool cool cool cool. So glad I found a way to make my life easier.

And to feel closer to Harold.

I kick a jug of chemicals. It rolls across the room and slams into the opposite wall.

This project was supposed to close the space that had been opening between us—space I don't know how to cross any other way. The good news is that Harold left such detailed plans behind, it won't be a problem to fix the rest of the room up. The bad news is that might be the last time I ever get help from my best friend.

Ms. H knocks on the door.

Hastily, I wipe tears from my eyes and jump up. But I can tell my face is all puffy. That assumption is proven beyond a doubt when Ms. H opens the door and looks down at me, her face melting into an expression of pure pity.

"So . . . how are things?"

I laugh and take a deep breath. "Been better."

"Wanna talk about it?"

My mind's still spinning. I just shake my head.

Ms. H nods. She scans the room. "Wow. You got a lot done. Listen—I have to get back to my class. But consider this dark corner yours to hide in, as long as you need. If you want to talk, about anything, you know where to find me."

Her sensing that I need a few minutes alone is just as good as sitting down for a heart-to-heart right now. I give her a watery smile.

I screw the red light bulb into the ceiling, fill the appropriate tubs with the appropriate liquids, and affix a foam pad to the bottom of the door to block any stray light. By Jove, we've got a darkroom.

Well, *I* have a darkroom.

Abandoning the suitcase for now, I march out of the dome a few minutes before the bell rings. Outside, I'm greeted by the singular, piercing sound of a group of people unable to find a common note. I peer around the corner. A group of freshmen stand in a line, shifting uncomfortably. Jaz Clarke stands in front of them like a drill sergeant in a floral dress.

"No, no, no. It's an A. Ever heard of it?" She sighs. "Just listen again."

Jaz clears her throat, stands up straight, and sings into the midmorning. She has the loveliest, clearest voice I've ever heard in real life.

But her how-it's-done lesson is over all too soon, and then the shoddy excuse for an a capella group launches back into atonal cacophony. And yet, it feels somehow appropriate. That's the world right now: out of tune.

CHAPTER 19

The group project to design the art dome space—and the actual construction on the art dome space—has distracted Ms. H so much that we've gotten a lengthy reprieve on the graffiti art assignment. That's the good news.

The bad news is it's been on the backburner for so long, I got distracted by another random act of kindness gift (this time for Loretta) and completely spaced. Again.

The morning the assignment is due, I wake up flying out of bed, stress at a peak before I even blink eye crust away. I fumble through the canvases propped in the corner of my room and paw through the envelopes of developed prints. As the fog of sleep lifts, it occurs to me that my concept for the assignment is not too dissimilar from a photo I took a couple of months ago.

I took the picture one afternoon, when I found Harold sifting through a stack of *New Yorker* magazines. He sat on the edge of his bed, almost directly in the center of the newspaper wall. The angle of sunlight gave the clippings' curled edges vicious, pointed shadows. I centered Harold in the frame. Tilting the camera just so, I got a perspective that made it look like all the news of the world was weighing on him.

Flipping through picture after picture of Harold is a pretty screwy way to start my day. It's been radio silence for the last week, since our darkroom blowup. It isn't that we've never fought before. But the last time I've gone seven consecutive days without so much as texting my best friend, I was still shopping at Gap Kids.

Won't lie—I had to reapply my eye makeup before I left the house. I would have said the hell with it, but I can't afford to just miss an assignment if I want to be a part of the showcase.

I buy a jumbo chocolate chip cookie at lunch to treat myself. Every other art class is held in the dome now. Though the space is a little chaotic, it has become more welcoming with the addition of random throw pillows and a seating area of overlapping beach blankets. The few beach chairs scattered around always seem to be claimed by the time I get to the Z wing. During school hours, skylights brighten the room. But several strings of twinkling fairy lights have been strung along the walls, too, giving the room a rich, warm glow.

When we arrive, a folding table has been set up. Ms. H sits beside it in a rolling desk chair. "Everybody take a seat, quickly," she says. "We need every minute to present your work."

Nate claims his favorite beach blanket, the one with Sonic the Hedgehog on it. He's sitting crisscross, chin resting on his hands. He's set his backpack next to him to save me a space.

"Hey," I say.

With a start, like waking from a dream, Nate stirs and looks at me. "Oh. Hey."

"Thanks for saving the seat."

"Of course." Nate grins.

Of course. I love how confidently he says it. Like, *duh! We frands!* I feel warm 'n' fuzzy as I sit down, leaning against my bag.

Ms. H stands from the rolling desk chair. "Who wants to go first?" Ms. H stares down at us. She scans the crowd. Alarmingly, her eyes finally rest on me. "Ivy?"

Uh . . . "Yeah?"

Ms. H's expectant stare makes it clear I must get up in front of the class and answer for my art. *GULP* doesn't begin to describe it. At least holding the graffiti print and my photo of Harold gives me something to do while I wither under the collective stares of a dome full of art students. Last year we turned in assignments and they all but disappeared, lost somewhere in the stack of things on Mr. Nguyen's desk. In a way, it was freeing to create something and send it into the ether. I could be proud of it, or I could forget about it and move on.

This year was going to be different. Harold's words echoed in my mind. *You can survive criticism. It's not actually life-threatening.*

Ms. H leans forward to examine my photo. "How was your portrait inspired by the graffiti you chose?"

"Well." I glance down at the graffiti. "This seems to be suggesting that the world is going down the drain."

"It does indeed," Ms. H agrees.

"There's no one I know of who cares more about all the things going wrong in the world than Harold Johnson. This is a portrait of him, sitting in front of a wall of his bedroom. Whenever Harold reads an article that's interesting, he cuts it out and adds it to the wall."

"So that background is not staged?"

I scoff. "No way, I would never be clever enough to even think of that. When I was sitting there with Harold, the light was changing. And there was this moment when I felt like his whole wall could come crashing down on us and it would be just, like, the most metaphorical way that two people could ever die. Literally crushed under the weight of the news of the world."

"And when you had that moment, you decided to take a picture."

"I don't really know what else to do with that feeling." I shrug.

"Did Harold know you were taking this picture of him?"

I start laughing and quickly rein it in. "Uh, no, nooooooo, no no no. Harold hates being photographed."

"You've taken lots of pictures of this subject?" Ms. H is real curious now.

"Oh yeah." I hold the picture out to her. "I mean, look at him." In the uncomfortable silence that follows, I realize what I've said. "Um. He's just really expressive. You know."

"Okay." She nods. I can tell she has questions that she isn't asking. "Why did you decide on black and white?"

She leads me through a few more questions about the photograph's composition, then blessedly I'm allowed to sit back down. Nate shifts stiffly away as I settle in, even though there's plenty of room on the blanket. I do a quick pit check—I sweated through my Wednesday Addams dress while giving that presentation. Maybe Nate is distancing himself from my malodorous anxiety. Ms. H calls on him next.

Nate heads to the side of the dome that is piled high with desks, stray chairs, an old-fashioned vacuum cleaner, and tons of art supplies in paper New Leaf Market bags. He fishes out a large portrait in a gold frame. The kind of painting that's at Value Village for, like, ten bucks.

The portrait depicts a figure leaning against an antique table. It's impossible to tell if the figure is a man or a woman or a deer dressed as a person because Nate has obscured it entirely, decoupaging it with bits of paper. Squinting, I can tell bits of paper are comments—some from VEIL, some from Twitter, or YouTube, or whatever. They're unmistakable, littered with hearts or thumbs or stars. He also holds up the artwork that inspired him: the man transforming as he plunges through a computer screen.

"Same question to you," Ms. H says. "How do you think your piece is inspired by the graffiti you chose?"

Nate's still avoiding looking at anyone, shifting uncomfortably. He considers the painting. "The graffiti is showing how someone can reinvent themselves online. Or, that's what I thought." He looks to Ms. H. She nods a silent reassurance. He takes a breath. "I had a lot of ideas about what to do for this prompt when we first got it. But some . . . things have happened since then. And it made me think about the graffiti differently. There's something missing from it, I think. Because yeah, you can go online and feel free to be yourself in a way that maybe isn't as acceptable in the real world. But you can also go online and be terrible. There are plenty of people who spend all their time online dragging other people down, and making assumptions based on such little information. Or no information."

Nate pauses. His neck is flush. Clearing his throat, Nate continues in a gruff voice. "The graffiti is all about freedom and beauty. I wanted to show the other side of that freedom, which is ugly. Even if it's only words."

The silence that falls in the dome is total. Everyone knows what Nate is talking about. Until now I'd mostly thought of Tag as the messed-up brother who dragged Nate, unfairly, into his angst. But now, with Nate staring at the ground while holding a portrait stand-in for his twin, it dawns on me in a whole new way that Nate and Tag are brothers, and friends. Even ignorant people who say hurtful things are human beings, with family and friends and hopes and things they care about.

It doesn't make me want to forgive Tag. But it does make me think about how he must be feeling. And wonder if, while he's at home, he's thinking as deeply about the people he hurt. We can only hope, I guess.

The rest of Nate's presentation goes smoothly. Ms. H obviously loves his work, and when he sits back down next to me, I detect the tiniest little proud smile. Though he still doesn't look my way.

Everyone else's work is interesting, but nothing tops Nate's portrait. I try a couple times to tap Nate's arm and get his attention, but am totally ignored. By the time the bell rings, I'm twisted in a jumbo pretzel trying to figure out if he's mad, and if so, why.

We get up and Nate shows no sign of saying goodbye. Panicked, I reach out and grab his hand. When he stares right in my face, his hand warm in mine, it feels like I've stuck my finger right in a socket. "What's wrong?"

"Nothing," Nate says lamely. At my *yeah right* expression he relents. "Just your friend Harold," he says, gesturing at my photo. "I bet you agree with him."

"Huh?" My genuine bewilderment gives Nate pause. He takes his hand back, but softens a bit.

"Harold. His editorial?"

Blank stare.

"Oh." Nate shakes his head. "Harold wrote an editorial in the *Belfry Bulletin* about Tag. I thought you knew."

"Hell nope," I say.

"I just want the whole thing to blow over, already. We all know what Tag said was wrong, and he got suspended and kicked off the team. Like, can we just move on?" He crosses his arms. "It isn't even like Harold's wrong, it just feels like salt in the wound, is all. And I didn't realize you were so close to him . . ." Nate hesitates. "Harold might hate Tag and, by extension, me. That's the price I pay, I guess. But . . . I don't want you hating me, too."

"Hate you?" I squeeze Nate's arm. "I could never. And I'm sure Harold doesn't hate you, either. What does his editorial say?"

Before Nate can answer, Ms. H approaches. "Ivy, can I steal you for a moment?"

I wave weakly at Nate as he excuses himself. He pauses in the doorway. I can only hope that lingering look means he believes me.

"I won't keep you long," Ms. H says, getting my attention. "But we have to talk about your photo for this assignment. It's not that it's a bad photograph. Quite the opposite, actually." She watches me carefully. "But Patton puts the date on the back of all his prints. That photo was taken months ago."

Busted.

"You're really talented, Ivy. I wouldn't offer a darkroom for a student I didn't believe in. But you're supposed to be creating new, original work for this class. That's the deal." I stare at the floor. When I finally look up, the awkward moment curdling in my gut, Ms. H is staring at me like I'm a sign written in a foreign language. "There's something holding you back," she says. "I'm not sure what it is. But it's something you're going to have to face head on if you want to realize your artistic potential."

Sucking a breath through my teeth, I smile at her. Because how are you supposed to respond to something like that? "Okay."

"All right, get outta here," she says. "You're gonna be late."

Don't have to tell me twice. After hightailing it out of the dome, I'm left blinking in the sunlight, with one thought clear as day: I've got to get a copy of the school paper and see what Harold wrote.

I head the opposite direction of my sixth-period class—toward the journalism lab.

CHAPTER 20

The journalism lab looks like it should hold rocket ships. It's a huge warehouse-style space with sky-high ceilings, all the ducts and pipes exposed. Good thing there's so much headspace, because the room is crammed with computers, photocopiers, stray photography equipment, stacks of reference books and encyclopedias, and—of course—a fancy coffee maker.

I've only been in here once before, as a freshman. After a massive pep talk from Harold, I brought in a few prints and an application to join the *Bulletin* as staff photographer. I'd stood in the doorway, ignored, trying to grab the attention of someone, anyone. Finally a harried senior made eye contact with me long enough for me to hand him my application, and the prints. He brushed me off and I let myself get brushed off, scampering out of the room as fast as my feet could shuffle. I wasn't surprised when I never heard back. If anything, I was relieved.

Today, though, I won't be scared away so easily.

In a corner, beside a bookshelf crammed with back issues of *National Geographic* and old yearbooks, is a desk with a plaque that reads: *MS. GOO.* She's the journalism teacher and *Bulletin* supervisor. Though NPR blasts from her speakers and a magazine sits open on her desk, the chair spinning behind the desk is empty.

The only other sound is the whirring of the photocopier, which spits out black-and-white copies at a rapid-fire pace.

"Hello?" I wander through the maze of tables, stepping over abandoned backpacks, duffel bags, and tangled cords. Copies of the *New York Times* and the *Washington Post* are strewn everywhere, but there's nary a hint of the *Bulletin*.

Turning back, I pass by the copier, then do a double take.

Across the top of each freshly printed page in the output tray, in familiar handwriting, is *BELFRY BARNACLE.* If life were a manga, an exclamation mark would appear over my head.

I grab the page. It's still warm. A half dozen headlines litter the crowded front page, including:

Competitive Air Guitar: An Illustrated Guide

and

Friendly Neighborhood Cult Insists There's Nothing to Fear

and

New Astrology Signs — It Isn't How You Live, But When

My favorite brand of *Barnacle* nonsense.

So, despite all their elaborate claims to the contrary, the *Bulletin* staff *is* responsible for the *Barnacle*. Ha! Or . . .

Everything from the still-spinning chair to the hastily thrown bags seems to indicate that the newsroom left, likely to go somewhere together. Leaning over the large table in the middle of the room, I place a hand on top of one of several stacked pizza boxes. It's still warm.

So, either the faculty advisor for the journalism lab has repeatedly lied to the administration, or someone with access to this room uses the copier whenever the *Bulletin* staff is looking the other way.

That makes sense, given what I've gleaned about the *Barnacle* creator from their posts on VEIL. The zinemaster has documented a meticulous work ethic. Everything from organizing the magazines they use for collages to the specific brand of stapler they use to bind the folded pages together are kept in labeled bins. Once or twice over the summer, they posted a marked-up version of the zine and talked about proofreading and developing a *Barnacle* style guide. This isn't a casual exercise by someone looking to distract themselves with faux rebellion; the *Barnacle* is something its creator takes seriously. Including, it seems, staking out the journo lab and pouncing on its equipment when no one's watching.

Folding the pilfered page, I tuck it in my pocket and move back to the door. A cardboard box props the door open. I lift one of its folded panels and: jackpot. It's packed with spanking new editions of the *Bulletin*.

"Can I help you?"

Heather Schusterman approaches the lab from the hall.

I hold up my copy of the *Bulletin*. "Just getting a paper."

Heather and I had advanced English together last year. We worked on a group project where we had to pitch *East of Eden* as a TV show, with a proposed cast and concept art for the setting. We spent a couple late nights at Heather's house, our things sprawled around her bedroom, binge-watching *Riverdale* "for research."

A few memories click into place. Heather's array of X-Acto knives and zeal for cutting things out of magazines to make a diorama of our setting—a glamorous Malibu beachfront community. She cut out easily three times as many images as we needed, and insisted on organizing the extra cutouts by category then carefully sliding them into plastic envelopes labeled with Sharpie and kept in a three-ring binder. She stored the binder in a craft closet, stuffed with labeled tubs of ribbons, scrapbook paper, Mod Podge, and twine.

Honestly, how many people in the world are that organized?

"See ya later." I step outside the lab. Heather passes me, going in. I linger just outside the door for a minute before peering back inside.

She hovers over the copier, holding a few of the freshly printed sheets in her hand. She flips through them, a satisfied smile on her face.

I can't help a grin as I speed-walk to the cafeteria.

So Heather is the genius behind the *Barnacle*. Will wonders never cease! I file that away next to the scoops I have on Loretta, Jaz, Jeanne, and Ajeet.

I'd be lying if I said I was in a rush to get to sixth period, given the mystery waiting for me in this copy of the *Bulletin*. So I sit on the cafeteria floor just inside the double doors and dive into the paper.

I flip to the second-to-last page, where they print student essays and analysis from the *Bulletin*'s editorial board. Let's just say this isn't the first time Harold's writing has appeared in the school paper. He's sent the staff about three dozen screeds on one thing or another over the last year. Ms. Goo probably dreams of the days when Harold Johnson was still in middle school.

There, above the fold on the Opinions page, is a column next to a black-and-white photo of Harold. It's an old picture: He looks bright-eyed and well-rested.

TIME FOR BELFRY STUDENTS TO COME INTO
THE LIGHT
By Harold Johnson

There's been much focus lately, and rightly so, on a post on the social media app VEIL that included homophobic language that upset many students at Belfry High. VEIL was founded as a kind of virtual artists' commune, but with a twist: All the artists could stay anonymous. This, founder Rake Burmkezerg says, allows for "unfettered creativity." But in the aftermath of the hurtful post, it seemed clear to me that some students are still desperately in need of fetters.

Many other students agreed. Now some of us are coming together to start Belfry's first ever chapter of the Pride Club, a group that welcomes members of all genders and sexualities, including cis-het allies. Though many VEIL users returned to that medium to post their outrage, anger, and frustration, I think something far more constructive can be found by banding together in real life—face-to-face. By throwing off the supposedly freeing shackle of anonymity, students can meet, peer-to-peer, and build a community of radical acceptance right here at BHS. Cowards can tap hateful speech onto a screen without much thought. It's much more difficult to look someone else in the eyes and tell them you don't respect their personhood.

Feminist scholars frequently cite a paraphrased quote from Virginia Woolf's essay "A Room of One's Own": "For most of history, Anonymous was a woman." Because of patriarchal societal pressures, women seeking to contribute to the arts, sciences, or politics, or in any way engage in important public questions of their day, were relegated to posing as "Anonymous," which many would have assumed to be coming from a male writer. Anonymous was a moniker adopted out of desperation, when no other avenue was possible.

Women, racial and ethnic minorities, and members of other marginalized groups are still under pressure to accept the systems that perpetuate their oppression. But in the 21st century, in a democracy, we have the right to stand up against those forces and speak our minds. By doing that, we can band together and reject the regressive forces trying to push their bigoted agendas on us. We can make it clear that Belfry is a safe place for students from marginalized populations in a way that can't be replicated on a screen. We have the right to speak using our real names, in real life.

The Pride Club will kick off by hosting a bake sale fund-raiser during lunch next Tuesday. The proceeds will be donated to the Parents of Belfry Legal Fund, founded to hold VEIL accountable for all forms of hate speech. All students, whether they identify as LGBTQIA+ or as allies, are invited to join us as we work to establish Belfry as a safe place where all students can thrive.

I fold the paper against my knees and lean my head back on the cool tiled wall. The editorial is so good, and just *so Harold*. I recognize bits and pieces from a few essays he wrote last year, and the unmistakable Speech and Debate tone he takes on when something gets him real riled up.

It isn't hard to see why hearing his twin brother called a "regressive force" trying to push a "bigoted agenda" would make Nate think Harold has major beef with at least one of the Gehrigs. The article fans the flames of a lot of ongoing controversies; reading it after the throwdown Harold and I just had about my choice to remain anonymous—even to VEIL—makes it feel like a kind of sideways attack.

It's also the perfect example of what makes it so hard to argue against Harold, or my parents, and probably everyone else associated with the Parents of Belfry Legal Fund: It's impossible to explain to some people what it's like not being brave. That "Anonymous" works today just like it did for women for centuries—by letting some people say what they want to say without having to be afraid. Afraid of both those who want to hold you down, and those who want to force you up before you're ready.

I show up a full fifteen minutes late to sixth period. I'll chalk this tardy up as yet another example of my own quiet rebellion.

CHAPTER 21

Developer fluid is thicker than water. When I tilt the tray, it sloshes back and forth in ripples that never become waves, covering the print evenly. My eyes, having adjusted to the darkroom's red glow, monitor subtle shifts of light as images on the print appear and darken. When it looks just right, I hurriedly remove the photo and set it in the stop bath. That neutralizes the development chemicals to keep the image just as dark or light, or underexposed or overexposed, as I want it.

Now that the darkroom is complete and construction is mostly done in the art dome, I'm using after-school studio time to experiment. After getting the hang of regular photo printing, I moved on to experimenting in the darkroom. The first step of today's project is developing one of my photos of a VEIL post. I chose one of Loretta's: She shot a bedroom wall covered in rectangles of lighter paint where framed pictures and posters used to hang. Below the empty wall is a headboard of metal twisted into curlicues, holding an uncovered mattress.

The test print turned out great—on the darker side of exposure, but that was on purpose. After it was dry, I cut up a spare piece of paper so that when I set it on top of the print, it limits the exposure to only the wall's rectangles of lighter paint. I expose a fresh piece of paper, then put my mask in place and flick the enlarger's light on again, projecting another picture onto the exposed squares.

It's the oldest photography trick in the book. You can do this—and so, so much more—with Photoshop in half a second. But dipping my fingers in chemicals, watching prints slowly emerge, cutting up the paper to cover bits of the print that I don't want double-exposed . . . The process makes it feel more real to me. It also allows for more mistakes, the serendipitous soul of art.

When I slip the print into the developer, the second photo emerges in the wall's rectangles. It's a photograph I took at one of the staircases built into the ocean cliffs. Someone had decorated the crumbling steps with rock towers: pebbles balanced so perfectly that they stay stacked, at least until some act of God—or a careless tourist—takes them down.

I've exposed the rock towers upside down, so the bare parts of the wall are full of menacing-looking stalactites. That, paired with the wrought-iron headboard, leaves a kind of sinister impression.

When the rock towers are as dark as I'd like them to get, I take the print from the chemical bath. After fixing and washing, I hang it up on one of the gently sagging wires that crisscross on the far wall. It'll dry next to a multi-exposure shot I made that's supposed to look like a sphere with waves on all sides and another that layers pictures of Painted Lady Day with shots of cliffs, making the Ancient Mariners look like they're sailing toward the edge of the earth.

But all my photo experiments so far have featured one or more of my pictures of VEIL posts, so no one besides me will see them. I try not to think of what Ms. H would say if she knew I was using studio time to make unoriginal prints.

I haven't been able to shake her come-to-Jesus talk. Part of me knows that messing around with VEIL posts—making art that I can never turn in for class credit—has to fall into the category of things holding me back. But in a way, what I'm doing with the VEIL posts is kind of like what Nate did with his painting. I feel like I'm putting my own stamp on the images—making a remix version, if you will. Sampling from others to make my own hit. Despite whatever Ms. H, or Patton, wants to think.

My hour is nearly up, so I clean the work area and shut the darkroom door behind me. I wave to Ms. H, who is helping Jason blend a watercolor at one of the newly erected easels. Outside, the day is bowing out in a citrus-colored blaze of glory. The last thing I want to do is go home. Staying late at school to take advantage of studio time has been amazing because I've gotten to play around with prints and development techniques, but if I'm being honest, it's also given me an excuse to avoid Parent Time. I dread finding Mom and Dad sitting on the couch, discussing their new favorite topic: VEIL. Every day they've seen a new interview with Burmkezerg, or read about an incident similar to the one at Belfry playing out somewhere else. They can't wait to tell me about it, and to parentsplain how the app works and what the dangers are and how little anything on it is policed for content. As if I don't understand the inner workings and the shortfalls of my favorite platform. Ew—*platform*? See?! Their constant chatter is already rotting my brain.

I decide to take a leisurely stroll around the Z wing. Now that I'm spending more time here, this part of campus has taken on a new charm. Most classes out here are electives, like journalism lab and musical theater. So on any given day you could stumble on someone staging a photo shoot for yearbook, flying a drone, or gutting a donated golf cart to turn it into a homecoming float. The domes and temporaries create a kind of maze. It's like Belfry's own version of Elbow's Temple, a place humming with promise of the unexpected.

Walking past the musical theater dome today, I catch the end of some kind of duet and the rippling of polite applause. Something's posted on the dome's door: a piece of paper announcing auditions for *1776*. Thinking immediately of Jaz, I run my finger down the list, checking to see when she'll be auditioning. This musical had been one of the many original cast recording vinyl records Jaz had taken pictures of and posted to VEIL this summer. But her name isn't there. I check a second and third time . . . no.

What the heck? Jaz has the voice of a friggin' angel. Her not auditioning would be like Harold joining a club but not signing up for some kind of leadership position. It just doesn't add up.

I wind through the buildings to the back bike rack where I've started parking Leibovitz. At this point in the afternoon, she's the only ride left. Tightening the helmet strap under my chin, I zoom off campus toward downtown.

It's nearly dark by the time I roll into the strip mall with Aperture Rapture and Beach Reads. I love seeing the bookstore lit up at night. In the dusk, its warm track lighting makes the face-out books look like rainbow jewels. The store is cozy and inviting, promising endless adventures.

The bell rings jauntily as I walk in, still slightly out of breath. Jaz stands behind the counter, gift wrapping a leather-bound volume of something or other. She's flailing, growing increasingly twisted inside of several strands of blue, yellow, and pink ribbon. Frustrated, she whips around and twists herself into a potentially deadly looking ribbon noose. I rush over and start pulling strands apart, freeing her slowly.

"Oh my god, thank you," Jaz says. Abandoning the ribbon, she takes out a decorative gift bag and tissue paper and begins stuffing the books inside. "So, what's up? You here to pick up Kristi's picks for this month?"

"Ah—well, yes. Also, I just happened to be walking by the theater today and saw that they're holding auditions for *1776*."

Tilting her head, Jaz examines me. "You thinking of signing up?"

I flap my hands. Even the thought of getting onstage and singing makes me feel like breaking out in volcano hives. "NO, no no no no no."

"Okay." Jaz looks down at her gift-wrapped books with a wounded expression.

"I mean, no, but I can't wait to see it. And I was looking to see when *you* were going to audition."

Jaz laughs like what I just said is completely ridiculous. "Nah. Mr. Ducca said he'd make me stage manager."

"Yeah, but—your voice."

"What about it?"

"It's, like, *good*. It's so good."

Jaz waves a hand dismissively. "Lots of people have good voices."

"Mmmmm, I dunno about that," I say, thinking of the a cappella group. "You love musicals. Don't you want to be onstage?"

Jaz looks puzzled. Just then arms wrap me up from behind.

"Darling!" It's Kristi. Even if I didn't recognize her bubbly voice or her gel nails filed to perilous points, I'd know by her signature scent: fresh books, old ink, and patchouli. It says a lot about my life that I know my neighborhood bookseller by smell.

"Hey, Kristi! I just wanted to show you something . . ." Unzipping my bag, I grab the most recent issue of the *Barnacle*—the one I discovered being pumped out of the journalism lab printer, but finished and bound. Kristi eyes the zine with one eyebrow curiously arched.

"What's this?"

"It's something my . . . friend makes, every month, and distributes at Belfry. It's like the *National Enquirer* for Sudden Cove—she's writing the funniest, smartest, weirdest stuff in there. And I was thinking about how sometimes independent bookstores sell local zines and, anyway. I wanted you to see it, and maybe you could consider selling them here."

Kristi gives me a "hmmm!" and holds the zine to her chest. "I will read it closely!" She blinks at me, and by the time I realize she's tearing up, it's too late to escape. "My favorite customer has reading recommendations for *me*," she says, pulling me in for another hug. "The student has become the teacher!"

Oh boy. "It's not a big deal, really, and if you don't want to carry it, no problem," I say into the arm of her enormous caftan.

Kristi just holds me tighter. "Fighting for Sudden Cove artists and writers. Drawing my attention to the lack of local, independently published work!"

"Um, Kristi, there's someone on line seven for you." Jaz holds the phone out with an expression of alarm.

Kristi gives me a final squeeze and marches off to the back room. "I'll be in touch soon, darling!" she shouts at me over her shoulder.

Jaz puts the phone down with a sly grin.

"There's no one on line seven, is there?" I ask.

"No." She glances toward the door. "And you better get out while you can."

I give her a quick salute. "I owe you one!"

When I get home, another lucky break: Mom and Dad have taken their after-work wine party to the back patio, and I'm able to sneak upstairs without a face-to-face confrontation. The sounds of *Tim and Eric's Billion Dollar Movie* from my bedroom are answer enough when they call me down to dinner.

Loretta has posted another image to VEIL. This one shows a stack of cardboard boxes piled in front of a Goodwill. Out of the top box poke two black button eyes and a velveteen ear. The caption: "Downsizing."

I'll take that as my sign to move Loretta's random act of kindness from the "plan" stage to fully in action. It's more ambitious and personal than Jeanne's, or even Ajeet's. But it feels right. Here goes nothing.

CHAPTER 22

I smooth out the frayed edges of the picnic blanket in the middle of the quad. It's no Sonic the Hedgehog, but the rainbow-colored Mexican blanket is what my family has always used for beach days. It fills me with memories of blue skies and coconut-scented sunscreen.

I hope some of that joy will transfer to my intended picnic companion: Loretta Kim.

It only took a folded five-dollar bill, exchanged in one sweaty handshake, to get Ron Thimble, the fourth-period office assistant, to get Loretta out of class. (Thanks for the idea, Harold.) Blessedly, office assistants aren't given ethics training before gaining access to half the resources that make this school tick. Rob passed her a note, scribbled on a ripped-out sheet of note-book paper: *Meet me in the quad for a picnic (I promise I won't serial murder you).*

I've laid out a spread that approximates the cheese platters my mom prepares when we have new grad students over. Hers has an almost tropical color palette, with carrots and broccoli and artichokes and cherry tomatoes and several wheels of cheese.

Mine has sliced hot dogs, string cheese sticks cut into little squares, butter crackers, slices of pepperoni, and Flamin' Hot Cheetos. I've set out a carton of chocolate milk for each of us, too. A little déclassé, perhaps, but it looks friggin' delicious.

I've already finished half my chocolate milk when Loretta emerges from the B wing, holding the note and scanning the quad warily. I wave her over and suck down the rest of the chocolate milk. I was so worried about the blanket and the picnic spread, I haven't fully prepared myself for when Loretta sits down across from me, crisscross.

"What is this?" Loretta eyes the food like it might jump out and attack her.

"A cheese plate."

She examines the plate, mildly impressed. "So, I got your note. Way to sound exactly like a serial murderer."

I sigh. "Turns out it's hard to get 'I'm not creepy' across in a genuinely uncreepy way."

"What's up?" Loretta grabs a handful of Cheetos and a few string cheese squares.

Taking a deep breath, I stare at the rainbow weave of the blanket and dive in. "I wanted to tell you that I know who you are on VEIL. The black-and-white pictures you've been posting all summer. And that what you're going through seems really hard and awful, but your art about it has been amazing."

Loretta pauses with a Cheeto halfway to her mouth. Orange flecks speckle her teeth. "How do you know that?"

"I saw you and your parents, outside the courthouse."

Loretta blanches. She sets the Cheeto down. "That was in the middle of the day."

"I know," I say, abashed. "I cut school that day. With Nate."

"What's up with you two, anyway?" Loretta raises an eyebrow. "Are you completely insanely in love with a football player?" Her voice lilts in a kind of singsongy way that suggests she's half joking. But the look on her face is deadly serious.

I shrug, cheeks burning. "I don't know. He's just really nice." I pick at the edge of the blanket before the reason for this picnic comes rocketing back to me. "Anyway, that doesn't matter. I want to talk about you."

"You want to pry, you mean."

"What?" I lean back, stunned. "No. That isn't—listen. I've been on VEIL all summer. And since school started, I've happened across some clues as to who some posters are. And, I don't know. I just wanted to tell them all what their work has meant to me." Reaching into my bag, I carefully extract a small canvas swaddled in tissue paper.

Loretta unwraps the paper carefully.

It's another painting. This one took me from *The Life Aquatic with Steve Zissou* to *Adam Resurrected* to finish. It's a re-creation of one of Loretta's pictures from this summer. The shot frames a bathroom: shower with no curtain, toilet with a strip of paper binding the lid closed, and a set of toiletry samples beside the sink. It's in black and white, like all the rest of Loretta's posts, but I imagine every tile in that space is the kind of pale pink that makes you think you smell talcum powder and Sensodyne.

That's how I painted it. Pink and mango and old and fussy, with the feeling of a cheap motel, rather than someplace Loretta was expected to claim as her own (every other weekend, at least).

Loretta covers half her face with a hand, her lashes growing thick and wet with tears. Her hair falls out of its messy bun and masks her blotchy pink cheeks. "This was before he told me he'd gotten me into art camp," she says. "I remember thinking that any camp tent, any bug-infested cabin, would be better than that dump." She takes a breath. "But it was the best he could do on short notice."

"How was camp?" I ask.

Loretta lets out a cruel, dismissive *humph* of a laugh. "It was great. Wonderful. Life-changing." Her tone suggests otherwise. She shakes her head. "It was prestigious. A recommendation from them will get me into the Rhode Island School of Design, for sure. Mom and Dad got themselves worked up over who could frame my work from camp the fastest, and hang it all over their houses." She turns the art around. "He doesn't live here anymore," she tells me, defensive.

"Do you like where he lives now?"

Loretta pauses, as though she'd been ready to answer a different question. Her shoulders unfurl and she sets the art down.

"Yeah," she says. "He got a place, a condo, up on the hill. By the college. It's really green, and you can watch the sun set from the deck."

I smile encouragingly. In my mind, I picture sitting on a deck with my dad, in a condo, trying to feel enough positive energy to make up for the fact that Mom wasn't there and never would be. I simply can't imagine it. My heart breaks all the way for Loretta Kim.

In my rush of feeling, I blurt out something I'd never say otherwise: "I was jealous that you got to go to art camp."

Loretta laughs. She doesn't seem surprised. "Yeah. It's fancy, and full of people who think they're the next Andy Warhol. Every kid with a trust fund and a whiff of talent shows up ready to cut each other down." In the falsely chipper voice of an infomercial, she says, "Camp Fussypants, where you'll make the friends, *and* enemies, you'll have for the rest of your life." She shakes her head. "I'm jealous of *you*, and everyone else who got to stay home and hang out with their families all summer. And you—" She pauses for a second, then continues: "Your art. It seems like you're still having fun. I can see the joy in it. I miss that."

I never thought a compliment from an art punk would make me blush. To be honest, I never thought I'd get a compliment from an art punk. "I always thought you hated me. Or at the very least, didn't like me."

Loretta considers me. "I haven't had the energy to hate anyone in a long time. The way I've always felt about you is . . .

neutral. Your art isn't bad. But you're so quiet, you know?" She leans in with a skeptical expression. "It isn't like you made an effort to get to know me. If you walk around thinking everyone's actions are always about you, life's gonna get real tiring, real fast." Loretta sits back on her hands, looking over the picnic blanket spread. "So. Why do all this?"

"Well, my parents didn't get divorced and I wasn't embroiled in art camp drama, but I had a hard summer, too," I say. "And following VEIL honestly got me through it. Now, with all this . . ." I frown.

"Chicanery?" Loretta suggests.

"Yeah. With all of whatever-that-is going on, I wanted to do something to make people feel better. Appreciated. So I kept my eyes open and have been trying to do little acts of kindness whenever I discover someone from VEIL."

Loretta narrows her eyes. "Wait a second. Were you . . . ?"

"The brushes for Jeanne?"

"Oh dang." The color rushes out of her face. "I wondered who did that."

I press my lips together and look down, waiting in the uncomfortable silence. She sits up. "I forgot Jeanne's birthday this summer, with everything going on. Not that that excuses it. She was really mad at me. When those brushes appeared, and she assumed I'd gotten them for her . . ."

I wave a hand. "It's fine."

"No, we can tell her—"

"Seriously." I look Loretta right in the eye. All the time I've stewed over Loretta taking credit for my thoughtfulness, all the dagger stares I've directed her way—suddenly all that built-up anger just . . . disappears. Evaporates, like the morning cloud cover that only needs a gentle breeze to break apart. "I don't want to tell her. That isn't really the point of this whole thing."

"You would give me this without telling me you painted it?" Loretta holds up the painting.

Hmm. "No," I say after a moment. "But this feels different." Buying the paintbrushes for Jeanne had felt good, but it was impersonal. For the fun of the surprise. But the paintings— first for Ajeet and now for Loretta—those I want to take owner-ship of.

Is this how people who regularly post on VEIL feel when they get upvotes? I have to believe this is better. Either way, I can't help but think, *Harold would be proud of me right now.* Of course, because it's Harold, he'd also say, "I told you so."

I miss him. All of him—even the petty parts.

The thought makes me tear up a little. I mess with my hair to hide my face.

"Well, dang," Loretta says, admiration in her tone. "So you're a regular VEIL sleuth, huh? What about that poet, the one struggling to come out of the closet? Have you sussed that one out?"

"No!" I say, frustrated. "I wish."

"Ah, well. Everyone's dying to know—I'm sure it'll come to light sooner or later," she says. "So who are you on VEIL? What would I remember?"

"Oh, I haven't ever actually posted anything."

Loretta looks stunned. "What? You're so into the app that you followed it all summer and bothered to paint something I posted, but you aren't putting up anything of your own?" She blinks once or twice, then shakes her head. "I can't tell if that's the coolest or the most deranged thing I've ever heard."

I scoff. "You sound like Harold."

"Speaking of . . ." Loretta looks over my shoulder.

Harold and a handful of others carry a long folding table to the edge of the quad. They set it up and unfurl a long banner: PRIDE CLUB BAKE SALE!

Harold glances over and does a double take, nearly dropping the banner. I see the calculation in his mind: ignore me and drive the wedge further between us, or do the grown-up thing and make some kind of truce.

I channel every ounce of energy in his direction, willing him to walk over.

He hands the banner to another club member and heads toward us.

"Hey . . ."

His hesitation about whether or not to hug me is obvious. But, now that I'm closer to him than I've been in what feels like weeks, I can't keep myself from wrapping an arm around his waist. He holds me tight and breathes out in relief. "Hey." A hug can't heal everything, but it's a pretty good way of saying we aren't enemies just because of one fight. Especially since he might have been a tiny bit right.

"Camping out for first dibs at the bake sale?" Harold asks.

"Uh . . ." I smile sheepishly. "Not exactly?"

"I'm super excited about it, though," Loretta chimes in. "I'm Loretta, by the way."

"Nice to meet you." Harold shakes her hand, because of course Harold Johnson shakes people's hands. He gives me one of the grins that I took for granted until recently. And, though he still looks too thin and tired, he's glowing. PBS fund-raisers have never charitied as do-goodily as Harold Johnson right now. He's in his element. "Well, I have to go help set up." He looks reluctant.

"Go!" I tell him. "Go, do good. I'll get in line ASAP."

He hurries away.

"He is *so* cute."

Loretta's declaration snaps me out of a daze. "Huh?!"

"He's a babe. Duh." She looks at me like I've got a screw loose. "Oh, sorry—are you two . . . ?"

"Uh, no." I start to pack up the picnic spread, trying to push down thoughts that bubble to the surface. Memories of backyard igloos.

Loretta watches me, amused. "Well then. I'll have to check

out this bake sale. Or—wait." She looks to Harold, where he's helping Andrew Appelhans unpack pink donut boxes with a metal cashbox tucked under his arm. "Is he gay?"

I drop the picnic platter. Hot dog slices fly everywhere. "What?"

"Is he gay?" Loretta repeats. "I mean, he did start the Pride Club. Not to make assumptions."

Forgetting the scattered spread, I watch Harold unpack rainbow-colored streamers. I thought I'd felt something, in the igloo. But based on his non-acknowledgment of that moment, and the fact that he's happier setting up the Pride Club than he's been in months . . .

And the op-ed! *We have the right to speak using our real names, in real life.* Couldn't that mean . . . ?

My shoulders fall. Understanding hits me like a truck.

If Harold is gay, that would explain why he's ignored our moment in the igloo, and why he responded so quickly and vehemently to the VEIL post. It might even be why he was upset about VEIL in the first place. If he feels like he's had to hide who he is this whole time, an added layer of anonymity could have felt like too much to handle.

Harold. Hiding who he's been this whole time.

The thought flattens me.

We've been best friends since he sat at my dinner table in fourth grade. I've told him about how looking at pictures of things with lots of holes, like honeycombs, makes me feel nauseous. I told him when I got my period for the first time. I've told him how sometimes I'm worried that my parents love each other more than they love me.

I'd always assumed Harold was being just as honest with me. It never, not for a minute, occurred to me that he would be hiding something this essential to who he is.

My mind races, thinking of reasons he might have kept this a secret. What have I done to show Harold that I'm not trustworthy? That I would judge him if he admitted he was gay, or questioning?

Then Loretta's words ring in my ears like a clarion bell: *If you think everyone's actions are all about you, life's gonna get real tiring, real fast.*

This isn't about me.

Harold chose not to tell me, and that's okay.

But now that I've figured it out, it's up to me how to respond. I want to find a way to tell Harold that I love him so much, for exactly who he is, and I always will.

This feels like the energy that comes from planning a random act of kindness, except ten times more intense. And with ten times the stakes.

I'll make this a random act for the record books.

CHAPTER 23

I'm still smiling from the high of Harold's lunchtime hug when I shove open the cafeteria doors to the Z wing and see Nate leaning against the art dome. I feel a jolt like I missed a step. He locks eyes with me. When I'm close enough to talk without shouting, he gives me a sheepish smile and holds out a folded paper. It's the *Bulletin*.

"Yeah, I read it," I tell him.

"Not this one." His eyes hold some kind of secret. "Try the op-ed page again."

Nervously, I flip the paper open and thumb to the page where Harold's editorial is printed. In the center of the op-ed section, Nate has taped a handwritten note:

To Whom It May Concern (Ivy):
I made a big mistake. I read Harold's article and I got upset. But my family's problems aren't yours. I am really sorry. I shouldn't have said those things and I hope you can forgive me.
~Contrite in Sudden Cove (Nate)

I fold the newspaper. When I look up, grinning like a little kid, Nate's relieved.

"What do you say?" he asks.

"Forgiven."

"Yeah?"

I swat at him playfully. "Yeah, you big goof." So long as he knows I don't hate him for what Tag said, and realizes anger isn't the right way to say he cares, we're good.

Nate makes a big show of wiping his forehead of faux sweat (perfect Nate Gehrig would NEVER truly sweat outside of hot football context). We fall into step walking toward Sonic the Hedgehog, chatting as easily as ever.

While Ms. H goes over a new assignment, I lean back on my hands and let it really sink in. Though my feelings toward Nate are still messy and unclear, the brief period when it looked like we might not be friends anymore was enough to prove one thing: I care about this sentimental jock a whole bunch.

A handful of students are presenting their interpretation of our most recent assignment, reflections on "Home." Loretta's up first, but she's uncharacteristically hesitant to get up when Ms. H calls her name. Jeanne gives her a reassuring squeeze, and the queen of the art punks looks almost bashful as she steps in front of the class with a few large prints.

Loretta takes a steadying breath and holds the first print up. It's a black-and-white image of a bedroom with oddly plain furniture. That isn't the only thing that's off about the furniture: Everything from the bed to the armoire has been cut in half.

"I found my old dollhouse this summer," Loretta says. "And I bought new accessories to experiment with these shots." The second print is of a room divided into light and dark, with a doll lying where the shadow cuts her in two. The third and fourth shots play with similar visual themes. Themes I'm used to seeing Loretta experiment with—but on VEIL. "This summer, my parents got divorced. I haven't turned in anything in this class that deals with that. I guess I didn't feel brave enough. But someone recently gave me a confidence boost."

She pauses for a breath. Briefly, Loretta meets my eyes. It's long enough for me to give her an encouraging nod. "So I decided the dollhouse gave me the chance to control the light, and to mess with the furniture and the interior of the house. It was actually really fun and productive."

Ms. H asks Loretta a lot more questions while the prints get passed around. Examining each one carefully, I feel a mix of appreciation, happiness, and pride. If I played even a tiny role in inspiring Loretta to bring this kind of amazing work into class, well. That just proves that the random acts of kindness are worthwhile.

"What do you mean, you've never heard of a panopticon?" I shake my head at Nate in disgust. "Do I have to educate you about every creepy thing?"

"I think it says a lot more that you *do* know all these creepy things, honestly." Nate's lying on Sonic, feet resting on a plush beanbag chair. I'm stretched out across the blanket beside him. The presentations have ended and we're supposed to be brainstorming a joint project, but Nate made some passing reference to the art studio being the set of a reality TV show, and that led me to go off on how much better the British *Big Brother* show is than the American version. Yadda yadda yadda, panopticon.

"Here, I'll show you." I grab my bag and dig out the sketchbook.

Nate lifts his legs off the beanbag and rolls onto his side. He watches as I flip through, trying to find any small blank corner to sketch in.

"Wait—" Nate presses down on one of the pages. "What is that?"

With a flick of his hand, Nate opens the sketchbook to one of several early drafts of my drawing of Loretta's post.

My chest constricts. "Um, a drawing?"

Nate examines the drawing more closely. "I recognize it. Is that . . ."

I shove his hand off the page and flip to the very end of the book. A page sure to be creamy white and free of any incriminating sketches.

He looks more amused than angry. "That was something from VEIL. From earlier this summer. Right?"

"I can neither confirm nor deny the inspiration for that sketch."

"Why are you drawing that?"

"You recognized it," I say defensively. "If we both remember a VEIL post, that's because it was really good. And now it's gone forever. I love VEIL, but I hate losing things like that. So I wanted to draw it—so it could be in my life a little longer."

"Wow." Nate considers this. "That's a very sweet way to think about it. Can I see it again?"

I hesitate for a moment, then flip back to the drawing. "It was one of my favorites," I say absently, smoothing the fraying corner of the page.

"Me too," he says. "Are there more?" His hazel eyes are so clear, his stare so direct, his face so close. Mere weeks ago, Nate Gehrig was a creature so beautiful and remote from my life, he may as well have been a centaur. I would've laughed at the idea that he'd ever know my name. Now he's asking permission to see more of my art, and observing it with something like reverence. My heart skips a beat or three as I spin the sketchbook around, placing it in his hands. "Sure." I shrug as if this is all no big deal. "There's a few more in there. I think."

There are drawings of exactly four more VEIL posts, several iterations of each, and a few dozen sketches of the double-exposure photographs I want to create. It takes a few tries to get the proportions right, and the shading just so.

Nate examines page after page, a smile playing at the edges of his lips. While he studies my art, I study the way his eyelashes grow so pale at the ends that they disappear, and how I can tell he needs a haircut because of the unruly curls at the base of his neck.

I can't believe how close I am—physically and, like, *emotionally*—to Nate Gehrig right now. But, somehow, it only makes me think more about my oldest friend. The short waves that form when he skips a haircut. How, even though he got contacts in ninth grade, Harold still shoves the ghost of his thick black frames up on the bridge of his nose when he's perplexed. How when he looks at my work he sees limitless potential. All the silly little details I know about Harold—yet I overlooked something so huge.

A plan for a grand gesture has been bubbling in the back of my mind. I think I know how to show both that I love him and fully accept who he is, all in one grand gesture. There should be a crowd—people who also want to thank Harold for everything he's done. And it has to be clear that when we say love, we mean it unconditionally. It kind of is an anniversary party, the more I think of it: a celebration of the year that Harold has been at Belfry, and how much he's managed to change it in such a short period of time.

It'll put the igloo to shame.

As for Nate, and these feelings for him . . . "I'm not just sketching these," I blurt out.

"Huh?" Nate turns his face up to mine.

I lower my eyes, cheeks burning. Now it's out there and I can't take it back. "These sketches. They're my first drafts. I've finished some of them, on canvas, or in the darkroom."

"Why?"

"Because they're pretty?"

Nate shakes his head. "No—these have so much detail, you've spent so much time. And you haven't turned in anything like this in class. There's something *up* here."

Folding my hands in my lap, I take a breath. "Well, I've given a couple of them away. To the people who posted the original images."

"People who originally posted the images to VEIL?" He pauses. "Wait. How did you find out who they were?"

I shrug. "I paid attention."

Nate's amused grin disappears. His expression darkens to concern and something else, something I can't read. "Whose pictures have you drawn?"

"Well, that first one, that's Loretta." Briefly, I glance over to the corner where Loretta and Jeanne are working on their project together. They're oblivious to our conversation.

"How did you know that picture was her?"

"Remember when we skipped class?"

"And we saw her at the courthouse," he mutters.

"She took a picture there, and it was up on VEIL later. And the composition of the photo, the fact that it was black and white, told me that Loretta had been the one putting up those images all summer. Plus, the person who posted all those pictures was obviously dealing with their parents' divorce, and in front of the courthouse, it was pretty clear that's the boat Loretta is in."

"You know . . ." Nate looks down at the drawings, running a hand lightly over the sweeping lines. "There's a reason Loretta put those things up on VEIL, where she could stay anonymous."

"I know. But if I was able to find out so easily . . ."

"We just happened to be skipping class and see her there. It doesn't really count as 'easy' that way—it was kind of stalkerish, if you think about it. And that was a private moment for Loretta and her family, you know?" He shuts the sketchbook, hard. "Did you ever stop to think that just because you *could* figure out who posted something on VEIL doesn't mean you *should*?"

Nate's getting upset. My whole body feels hot. I reach for the sketchbook. Nate shoves it in my direction.

"Just think about it next time, before you get all Rake Burmkezerg on someone."

I recoil, clutching the sketchbook to my chest. "I didn't . . . I'm not . . ."

Nate pinches his nose. "Sorry," he says, gruff, gathering his things. "I'm just upset in general. The Tag thing just isn't going away, and this"—he indicates the sketchbook, or maybe he just means me—"isn't helping."

He throws his bag over one shoulder, mutters something to Ms. H about the bathroom, and leaves. There's twenty minutes remaining in class, but something tells me Nate won't be back. I'm left stunned, trying to grasp what just happened. He went from thinking my random acts of kindness were sweet to thinking it made me no better than Rake Burmkezerg selling out Tag's identity. So much for being honest.

Ms. H looks after Nate as the door shuts behind him. She sits beside me, legs crossed. I'm reminded how young she is, barely more than a student herself. "What's up with him?"

I shake my head. If I try to say anything, I'll start to cry. I take a deep, careful breath.

Ms. H leans in. "How are you?"

I let the breath out slowly. "Peachy."

"Nate's going through a tough time," Ms. H says, patting my knee gently. "I'm sure whatever he did or said, that he didn't mean to hurt you." She begins to get up, then pauses. "Actually, I did want to talk to you. Last time we spoke, you agreed to double down on effort for this class. Unfortunately, I'm still not seeing it. I know for a fact you're capable of more inspired work." Ms. H eyes me carefully, like she's waiting for me to give something away. "Aren't you interested in being part of the semester showcase?"

"Of course."

"Well, I'm not seeing that with the level of work you're turning in," Ms. H says.

Damn. This lady is not playin'.

But, like, could she have possibly chosen a worse time to drop truth bombs? The tears do more than threaten this time. I duck my head to wipe them away.

"I don't mean to be hurtful," Ms. H says. "But I think this is the best way to get through to you. I see your energy directed elsewhere, and I don't understand it. You have a great gift. Let me help you develop it."

I just nod, staring at the edge of the blanket. When, when, when will this class please be over?

Ms. H gets up and pauses, weighing what to say. "Tough love is still love, you know?"

"Yeah," I say, weakly.

With a sigh, Ms. H moves on.

I grab my phone and retreat into the newest VEIL posts. We aren't supposed to use our phones in class but I dare someone to say something to me about it right now.

M aybe
O ne day
R eality will reflect outside
E verything I feel within.

T elling the truth seems
H erculean. How?
I

N ever expected such a little word:
G ay! Could
S care me so much.

C ourage is
H ard to find.
A nd those I thought might be able to help are
N ot who I thought, or hoped, they would be.
G rowing up; no one promised it'd be
E asy, but nobody told me it would be this hard.

The poem breaks my heart. And according to Loretta, I'm not the only one who wants to know who the poet is—to give them what little comfort I can. This is exactly the kind of person Harold had in mind when he started the Pride Club.

Wait.

Harold . . . The closeted poet . . . The Pride Club . . . Is it possible that Harold is the one who has been writing about being stuck in the closet? I shake the idea off. Harold was *so* against VEIL, in such a genuine way. I can't picture him posting there. Yet . . . ?

Ugh. I don't know! I don't know what to believe anymore. I feel so helpless.

The next post is from Jaz. I can tell because it's the same bedroom, with the same filters, showing a new record playing on the same old record player. The record this time: original cast recording of *1776*.

Stage manager my hangnail!

Harold shouldn't have to stay in the closet because he's scared. Jaz shouldn't have to accept a backstage part because she can't see that she's destined to be a star. Loretta just needed someone to say they understood to start coping with her parents' divorce. Like Ajeet, who only needed to be told his art was beautiful to feel like he could speak up about his summer fighting cancer.

I wait, impatient, for the bell to ring. Then, shoving past everyone to escape the dome, I march over to the musical theater building. I scribble a name in the very last audition slot:

Jasmine Clarke.

CHAPTER 24

Signing Jaz's name wasn't enough to curb my feelings of help-lessness. So, while I had momentum to spare, I decided it was time to act on another of my VEIL leads: Heather Schusterman.

It was a strange mental exercise to think of what would con-vince Heather Schusterman—badass subversive, über-organized go-getter whose zine exposes the dark underbelly (and weird conspiracy theories) of Belfry High—to meet with me at Beach Reads, sleepy local mom-and-pop shop.

"You didn't need to make a creepy threat to get me here," Heather says, walking through the games 'n' toys section toward me, waving my note in the air.

As an incentive to get Heather to show, I made a zine-inspired note. I realize now that by writing it with letters cut from maga-zines, I bypassed "zine-y" and went right to ransom note. And the message inside ("I know your secret. Be at Beach Reads at 5 and I'll share a surprise.") could be seen as outright murdery.

How did I not learn my lesson from Loretta's come-to-the-quad summons?!

Heather shakes her head. "I'm here every Tuesday, anyway, for the feminist book club. Duh." She gives me a wry smile. "Good thing I saw you shoving this in my locker, or I would have called the authorities. For sure."

"Ugh. I'm sorry." I cover my eyes. "I'm not aces at stealth."

Heather laughs. "Luckily for you, I've had people contact me in *way* stranger ways when they figure out I'm behind the *Barnacle*."

That pulls me up short. With a wave of her hand, Heather dismisses my surprise. "That's why you're reaching out to me, right? What is it—you got a scoop? You seem like one of those sit-in-the-corner-and-listen-to-everyone type of loners. I bet you have hella dirt."

Okay, first of all: That is true. Wallflowers have ears. And second of all: Dang! Heather Schusterman is *good*. "You got me," I admit. "But I'm not trying to feed you hot goss. Actually, I wanted you to meet . . ."

Just then, Kristi appears with a flourish, waving her massive caftan sleeve like she's in color guard. "Ivy!" She drapes an arm over my shoulder. "Is this our local Lois Lane?" She eyes Heather approvingly. "Heather Schusterman. I should have known." Turning to me, she says, "She's the one who insisted we add *Wide Sargasso Sea* to our book club list. Brilliant."

Heather smirks, looking pleased with herself.

Brandishing her sleeves like a matador herding bulls, Kristi ushers us to the secluded seating area behind the Romance section. We fall into the perfectly lumpy armchairs. Kristi perches on a loveseat's armrest. "Heather, it has been brought to my attention by one young intrepid reader"—she winks at me—"that your independent magazine, the *Barnacle*, has a wide readership and a reputation for . . . *innovative* content.

"It just so happens that Beach Reads is looking to support more local publications. I'd love to carry the *Barnacle*, if you think you can create new issues on a regular basis."

It's hard to read Heather's expression. With her, it's more than wheels turning: She's got a whole Rube Goldberg machine of interconnected thoughts whirring along. After a moment she sits up. "I've been thinking about the future of the *Barnacle* for a while," she says. "Expanding the staff, maybe covering more than just Belfry. So long as you don't make me change anything I put in the zine, you've got a deal." She sticks her hand out. Kristi, obviously delighted, takes it. They shake and I feel, for some reason, super relieved.

"Huzzah!" Kristi claps and stands. "Well, I have to get the coffee and cupcakes ready for book club. You're coming, right, Heather?"

"Wouldn't miss it."

"Ivy?" Kristi raises an eyebrow in my direction.

"Ah—not tonight," I hedge. The parking lot outside Beach Reads is washed in the yellow glow of the streetlights. The night air is cold and damp. Within the hour, all of Sudden Cove will be consumed in mist.

I stand beside Leibovitz and shut my eyes. I want to feel awash in self-satisfaction for the deal I just brokered between Heather and Kristi. And joy for Jaz's pending audition. But there's still this nagging something. This feeling that my real focus right now needs to be on Harold.

But I can't plan my grand gesture overnight—I just have to be patient.

Ugh.

I'm kneeled down by Leibovitz, turning on the string of twinkle lights that I've twisted around her frame for night riding, when the bookstore door swings open. Kristi looks relieved. "Thank god you're still here!" She holds out a Beach Reads bag bursting with books. "These are all for Harold. He hasn't been in for months and I can't keep holding his orders. Plus"—she levels a conspiratorial look at me—"from what Jaz tells me, I think there's a lot in here that Harold needs to hear right now."

Perfect. I hop up and grab the bag.

"I was just on my way to see him," I tell her, flashing a smile.

Kristi smiles, hands on her hips. "He's a special guy, Ivy. And he listens to you. Make sure he's doing okay."

I give her a salute and hop up on Leibovitz, glad for an excuse to head in Harold's direction.

Most of the route from Beach Reads to the Johnsons' is uphill. I'm pedaling like crazy, lights flashing through the murky evening.

The bag of Harold's books slides back and forth in the bike's basket at every tight turn.

When I get to his house, I hop off Leibovitz and walk the bike to the driveway. Then I notice something odd. The Johnsons' garage door is a carriage-style setup, which means the front opens from the middle, like French doors. Right now, one of the doors is propped halfway open. A faint blue light creeps onto the driveway.

Grabbing the book bag, I leave Leibovitz propped against the white picket fence and approach the garage.

The door creaks. My eyes adjust slowly to the garage's interior, pitch dark but for the faint glow of a cell phone screen. The Golf's passenger side doors are both open. Books and papers spill out of the front seat onto the floor. Harold stretches across the entire back seat, arms raised above his head as he scrolls on his phone.

"Hello?"

Harold yelps and sits up, banging his head against the car doorframe. I rush to see if he's okay. Clutching his head, Harold taps on the Golf's interior light. The bright yellow luminescence fills the garage. He rubs where his forehead met doorframe, and I get a glimpse of the dark circles under Harold's eyes. "What are you doing here?" he groans.

I shove him over so I can sit in the back seat beside him. "What are *you* doing here?" The car's interior is distressing. Pop-Tart wrappers, Clif Bars, uncapped Sharpies, and dozens of opened books. There's a toothbrush propped in the cup holder and several pairs of socks balled up in the passenger seat, on top of a crumpled blanket. "Are you, like, living here?"

"The house . . ." He sounds weary, like even talking is asking too much of him. "It feels so far away. Sometimes."

Okay, so there are some obvious questions that need asking. But Harold and I haven't been on the sturdiest footing lately, so it feels like baby steps are the right way to go. I pull the Beach Reads bag onto my lap. "I come bearing gifts."

Harold looks happy and anxious when he sees the logo on the bag. "Aw man, Kristi. I haven't been in for months."

"Don't think that has escaped her notice. She gave me these to drop off with you."

Harold has a familiar sparkle in his eye when he reaches into the bag. But his expression slowly darkens as he pulls the titles out, one by one.

Street Smart: Where College Fails Promising Young Minds, by Jacqueline Roosevelt.

The Obama Legacy: What Having a Community Organizer in the White House Taught Us, by Arlen Uzbaniak.

Silicon Valley Suicides: The Toll Start-Up Culture Took on a Generation of Palo Alto Teens, by Rebecca M. Alter and Jordan Pippin.

"Huh," Harold says, tossing the books back in the bag. "Not exactly subtle, is she?"

I shrug. Each title seems more and more applicable to Harold. I send a secret note of thanks out to the universe that someone like Kristi can get through to him using the one medium he trusts unreservedly: the written word.

But Harold is not pleased. "Everybody's got an opinion," he mutters.

"Maybe Kristi's just trying to tell you that there are more options out there for you."

Harold scoffs. "No offense, Ivy, but what does Kristi know about what I'm going through? Does she have my parents, with their expectations? Does she go to Belfry to see my competition? Does she have to work twice as hard to get half as far?"

"Wait—your competition?" I set the bag of books on the car floor. "Don't you mean your classmates?" There's a lot about this Harold situation that's disturbing. Like the fact that I may or may not be sitting on ketchup packets right now. But what Harold just said sets off more alarm bells than anything else. This is the guy who started ninth grade by finding the handful of people at BHS who were still playing Pokémon Go, then guiding them through the process of starting a club. This is the guy who organized carpools to get BHS students to protests outside Twitter's headquarters when they refused to block a lying politician. That "rising tide" aphorism is basically Harold Johnson's middle name. It's part of why I love him so much.

That's why hearing him talk about college in a mercenary way is so worrisome. It's all his parents' entrepreneurial tech-industry spirit, combined with a work ethic he just can't control, and more than a dash of the sky-high expectations—and accompanying pressures—that Smarty-Pants Campers drilled into him. He's driving forward at an unsustainable pace, and I'm afraid of what a crash would mean.

"No offense, Ivy. But you just don't have any idea what you're talking about." Harold leans his head back on the seat. We lapse into awkward silence.

"So, things seem . . . intense," I say.

"I'm working on it."

I shake my head. "I think you working is causing the problem."

"Some of us have responsibilities," Harold snaps. That shuts me up. He sighs. "I didn't mean . . . I just have a lot on my mind."

"And I don't?"

"Well, you aren't engaged the same way I am. If you have a bad day, what happens? Art class is less interesting? Ivy, you can't even bring yourself to post on an anonymous app. You don't know what it feels like to have people relying on you."

Harold's never talked to me this way. I step outside the car. "You think I'm hiding from my life? What do you call this?!" I gesture to the car, the garage, the cold black night. "You're living in the car! Too tired to walk twenty feet to your own bed! You have to learn how to say no sometimes," I tell him. "To school. To your parents. And maybe even to yourself."

Harold moves to the edge of the back seat, setting his feet on the garage floor. But in the middle of pushing himself to standing, he gives up, crumpling into a defeated hunch.

Maybe he doesn't think he can come out because he would disappoint someone. Anyone. He's so convinced that the world rests on his shoulders, he doesn't think he can trust the people around him to show up when he needs them.

"I'm worried about you, Harold. So is Kristi. Just . . . take a look at those books. And for god's sake, get some sleep."

My impulse is to help him to the house and tuck him into bed. But his words are a fresh wound on my heart. Harold Johnson isn't the only one with pride.

On the bike ride home, I start to move past that hurt. I keep thinking back to the picture of the newspaper wall looming over Harold—putting the weight of the world on his shoulders. That's how he feels, and he doesn't believe that people can give him space to just *be*.

I have to prove him wrong, before my best friend is gone forever.

CHAPTER 25

Marines have never gathered more efficiently than Sasha Oh when I ask her to help me plan a grand gesture for Harold. When she asks what it's for, all I have to say is, "To thank him for everything," and she gets it. "About time someone did that," she says.

"Well, that's what best friends are for," I say, breezing past the pang of fear that Sasha Oh—who sees him every single day—is going to call me out as no longer being Harold's BFF, based purely on lack of face time.

Instead, she looks me up and down and nods in what seems like approval. "I always doubted Harold when he told us stories about you."

"Why?"

She shrugs. "Wasn't convinced you were capable of speech."

I frown. "It's called being aloof."

"It's *called* social anxiety," Sasha says, pulling out a binder and immediately creating a to-do list for the party. "It's okay. I get it."

There are some highlights of working with Sasha. Most especially the look on her face when I reveal that *Love, Actually* is Harold's favorite movie. (He could go on forever about how problematic it is—but doves have never cried as mournfully as Harold at that little kid's airport surprise.) Her eyes widen and for a moment there is a genuine, honest-to-god smile. "That explains so much." Then she literally makes a note of it.

On the day of the party, we gather in the joined classrooms of Mr. Kuehn and Mrs. Maciel, who teach AP U.S. History to forty kids at a time. Sasha assured me we could get the space after school because that's where they hold Pride Club meetings.

"Trust me, we'll need the room," she says.

When I walk in, I gape at the size of the space. "You fill this whole place during Pride meetings?" I ask.

Sasha nods. "The first few were still standing-room only."

As I stand in front of the class, assessing how to decorate the gigantic room, I feel another pang. This is where Harold would have stood during the first Pride meeting, in front of a standing-room-only crowd of dozens ready to support his idea, and one another. And he didn't see his best friend's face in the crowd. I let him down.

Now's my chance to make up for it.

Sasha and a few more Pride members help me set up at lunch. We drape streamers, blow up balloons, and set out plates of store-bought cupcakes and chocolate chip cookies.

I'm still soaring high when I skip into art.

Until I see Nate, leaning on Sonic the Hedgehog. I falter, until Nate smiles at me.

"Not to sound like a broken record," he says as I sit beside him, "but sorry about last time. I'm just a mess."

Boy have I been there. And given my recent realization about how much I've disappointed someone I care about, I'm inclined to forgiveness. I tap my knee against his. "No worries."

"Well," he says. "You look ebullient."

I narrow my eyes. "What did you call me?"

Nate laughs. "Tag's going stir-crazy at home. He's taken to reading the dictionary and leaving his favorite words around the house. That one was on my mirror yesterday. It means cheerful and full of energy."

"Well then, you are right. I am ebullient."

"May I ask why?" he asks, putting on a formal tone.

"You may, but it's a bit of a surprise." I pause. "Actually, you should come. It's after school today—I'm doing something special for Harold."

At the mention of Harold, Nate's expression sours.

I rest a hand on his. A jolt courses through me. "I think it'll help you see where Harold is coming from. You should go. Really."

Nate's square jaw flexes while he considers. It's not distracting at all. Nope. "Well. We have a bye this weekend, so practice is only going to be a short film session."

"Perfect!" I clap. "Harold has Key Club till four o'clock, so it'll be after that."

"All right," Nate says, a little hesitant. The crease of concern he sometimes gets between his eyebrows is in full effect.

"Seriously," I assure him. "You won't regret it."

After the final bell rings, I pack up my things slowly and meander to my locker. I have an hour and a half to kill before Harold's party. How am I going to pass the time without going insane? Absently scrolling VEIL, I come across a post from someone preparing to audition for *1776*.

Jaz!

I make a strangled squealing sound, pocket my phone, and zoom off for the musical theater building. The entrance to the dome sits slightly ajar. Warbling wafts through the Z wing. Quietly, I slip into the dark theater.

A single spotlight illuminates the stage. Observers are scattered throughout the stadium-style seats. The head of the theater department, Mr. Ducca, is in the front row, a flat felt cap pulled down over his thinning hair. He sits cross-legged, rapidly scribbling notes on a clipboard. Onstage, a freshman girl wearing a Viking hat belts out something in . . . Italian, maybe? Klingon?

I settle into a seat in the far back. Mr. Ducca raises his hand.

Freshman Viking doesn't see, because her eyes are squeezed shut. She is *very* feeling herself. As far as I'm concerned, she's got a ten in style points.

Mr. Ducca stands up, trying to get through to her. "Vivienne," he says, then shouts. "Vivienne! Thank you! The audition is over!" Still nothing. He steps toward her, resting his hands on the lip of the stage. "Vivienne! Darling! Please stop!"

Vivienne gives a start, throwing her Viking hat askew. Her song cuts out with a nasal peal.

"Thank you," Mr. Ducca says gently. "You'll be hearing from us."

As Vivienne leaves the stage, Mr. Ducca sits back down, rubbing between his eyes. He pauses a moment, then flips his papers up. "Next up," he shouts, "Jasmine . . . Jaz?"

A buzz ripples through the small crowd. A blond girl in a black turtleneck pokes her head out of the backstage curtain. "Sorry, Mr. Ducca, but did you say *Jaz*?"

He holds up the audition sign-up sheet. "Her name's written right here."

"I'll find her." The girl looks excited as she drops the curtain closed behind her.

I pick up snippets of conversation from the seats around me.

". . . didn't know she could sing . . ."

". . . she mention to you that she was trying out?"

". . . can't be in the play *and* be stage manager, right?"

Finally, the backstage curtain shakes. There's a vague clamoring of people whispering loudly. The curtain parts and Jaz breaks through, heels first, like she's being shoved onstage.

"Jaz!" There's a smile in Mr. Ducca's voice. "I'm so excited you signed up!"

"Well, here's the thing—I didn't." Jaz's voice shakes.

"What's that?" he asks. "I can't hear you all the way over there. Move to the center of the stage, please."

Jaz steps gingerly across the boards, stepping into the circle of spotlight. She peers into the dark.

"Now what were you saying about not signing up?"

"That I didn't."

"Who would sign you up? And as what, some kind of joke?"

"I don't know!" Jaz insists.

"Well . . . since you're already there . . ." Mr. Ducca shrugs. "Why not just give it a shot?"

Jaz squirms. "I don't know . . ."

"Oh, come on," he says, drawling slightly. "Ain't nobody here but us chickens."

The theater goes still. I think everyone's doing the same thing: holding our breath and hoping. A few black-clad crew members gathered at the edge of the stage lean forward in anticipation.

"Well. I don't really have anything prepared . . ." Jaz stares down at her feet for a moment. Then she raises her head, opens her mouth, and unleashes a voice that would make angels cry. But listening to Jaz hit those incredibly high notes—hearing her rich voice fill out every word—is second only to the beauty of watching her perform. Her hands reach out, pull back, rise and fall as the song reaches its climax. Her eyes seem to have grown bigger, somehow, and they search every face in the theater, pleading with us to feel her emotion. This is some real Celine Dion stuff.

She's captivating.

When the song fades, Jaz closes her eyes.

I wipe away tears before joining the rest of the theater in rapturous applause. Our outpouring of love jolts Jaz into the present. She goes pale and stiff. Blinking rapidly, she backs up, turns, and runs from the stage, shoving past the crew members crowded by the curtain.

"Well." Mr. Ducca rises to face the audience. "I think it's fair to say we've found our John Adams. That's it for auditions—parts will be posted next week."

The house lights lift. As the audience filters to the exit, I head toward the stage, slipping behind the curtain. The crew members gather around Jaz, fawning over her with praise.

Jaz spots me and flushes. "Ivy? Ohmigod, you were out there, too?"

"You were amazing!"

Jaz tugs at her ear. "That was so wild. Like, adrenaline rush." She shakes her head. Then, slowly, she looks me over. "Wait a second."

Here we go.

"It was you. You signed me up, didn't you?"

"Well." I fight a smile. "First of all, congratulations on nailing the lead in the school musical. Secondly, yeah. I signed you up."

Medusa never stared as stone-turningly as Jaz looks at me right now. "Um, what?" she says, flabbergasted. "What is *wrong* with you?"

"I know it's you who's been posting all those photos of the musicals you were listening to, so I knew you loved them, and I knew you had a great voice . . ."

Jaz shakes her head in shock. "You figured out who I was on VEIL? And then you thought because I loved something so much, I wouldn't know that I wanted to audition?"

"Oh—well . . ."

"You know I'm the stage manager, right?" Jaz says. "First sophomore ever?"

"I mean . . ."

"And that being stage manager is kind of a big deal?"

"I just thought—"

"Did you?" Jaz asks. "Sounds more like a series of assumptions than a train of thought. I mean, listen—that felt really good out there. And maybe I wouldn't have gotten brave enough to try until next year. But that was also the scariest moment of my life. I'm still shaking." Jaz holds a hand out. True to her word, it trembles. Her whole arm is covered in goose bumps.

"But you nailed it," I say. "You looked so comfortable up there—a total natural."

"Neato. But let me tell you what I was actually feeling: totally *not* natural. My heart is still going a million miles a minute." Jaz shakes her head. "Listen, I don't know what to say. Thanks, I guess? But that was not cool."

My legs feel like jelly. I cross my arms, holding myself together. "I'm sorry, seriously. I was trying to do something nice."

"*Nice.*" Jaz rolls her eyes. "Got it. Listen, I'm gonna go celebrate with my friends now."

"Oh." I back up. "Right—of course." I rush out, desperate to escape this vortex of awkward. I navigate stray props and confusingly curtained halls to the back entrance, which I slam open to step into the school's rear driveway. The light is blinding. The sounds of conversation and distant honking are disorienting.

What just happened?

I thought this random act of kindness was the best one yet—Jaz's beautiful voice! Her obvious love for musicals! She deserves the lead (obviously!), and I just helped her see something she wouldn't have if left to her own devices. She just needed a little push, like Ajeet with talking about his diagnosis, or Loretta with sharing the pain from her parents' divorce, or Heather with expanding the reach of the *Barnacle*.

And Jaz nailed it. I mean, *nailed it*. Yet . . .

Her face when she realized I was the one who sprung that surprise audition on her—that was ice-cold. I may never warm up. I wander, unsteady, back toward the quad.

Harold's party.

Jaz's reaction throws me into a total tailspin. Up is down, left is right. Is Harold's party even a good idea?

Spots swirl in my vision; I'm struggling to catch a breath. I close my eyes. I go back over my reasoning, reminding myself why what I'm doing for Harold is the right thing. To help people like the closeted VEIL poet—who might also *be* Harold—and others who are desperate to be seen and loved for who they are.

And it's the Pride Club! It's a safe space. If Harold has been keeping his sexuality a secret even from me, someone he's cut his toenails in front of? Then he needs a big show of support to prove to him that we all love him because of who he is, not in spite of it. I've been too scared to be an active ally to this point, but that stops now.

It's good. It's gonna be great.

Plus, at this point, it's too late to call the party off.

I tighten the bun on top of my head and take a deep breath. Speed-walking to the AP U.S. History classroom, I stave off the flood of doubts by imagining Harold's surprise face. His glow, his childlike excitement, his glee.

That's worth risking almost anything.

Right?

CHAPTER 26

The AP U.S. History room is packed with various members from the Pride Club and student government. The 4-H Club brought tiny sliders. Model UN set out rows of cupcakes with little international flags stuck in each one. Curiously, Speech and Debate brought freshly brewed chamomile tea ("For the throat," Monica Ghofrania explains). It warms my heart to see all the people milling around just for the chance to tell Harold how much he means to them. There's even a representative here from Comic Book Club, and all Harold did for them was figure out what images they could put on their website without getting sued by Stan Lee.

I spot someone in the corner who sends my heart rate flying: Nate. The fact that he trusted me enough to come is amazing.

"There you are," Sasha says.

"Yeah, sorry." I smooth my hair and take a deep breath. *Focus, focus, focus. This is about Harold!* "Is he on his way?"

"Should be."

Running to my bag, I grab a curled-up posterboard. It was last weekend's project. Just because I'm throwing a big party for

Harold doesn't mean I want to skip the more personal artwork element. I wanted to make something for Harold every bit as special as what I made for Ajeet and Loretta.

The posterboard is entirely covered with pictures either of Harold, or that remind me of him. I went to Copier Comrade and reprinted dozens of photos, cut them out, and Mod Podged them to create the background. Then, I handwrote an original poem and pasted that on top.

It reads:

H ero to many
A lly to all
R ight now you're carrying burdens all
O n your own
L et us help you. Let us love you, the way you
so richly
D eserve.

I stride to the front of the room. "Hey." I'm trying not to melt under the blazing stares of forty-plus pairs of eyes. "Um, I'm Ivy. Sasha helped me plan this event for Harold. I would say that I can't believe this many people are here to tell him thank you for everything, but honestly? It's Harold. The whole world could show up and this could turn into Live Aid and I wouldn't be surprised."

Sasha laughs.

"What's Live Aid?" Brandy Fitch asks Andrew Appelhans.

"Everyone get ready to do the corny 'Surprise!' thing," I say. "Trust me. He's going to love it."

Helping the VEIL posters I discovered was so satisfying. But there's no doubt that this is going to be the best thing I do this year. My chest is tight, and the butterflies in my stomach are fluttering so hard I feel mildly nauseous. Harold told me that when he gets nervous, like before a Speech and Debate competition, he feels like he really has to pee. That's when he knows he's really ready. Maybe wanting to vomit and pass out is my version of "ready."

Harold's voice rumbles from outside the door. The knob turns and Harold walks through the door with his effortless swagger.

"Surprise!"

The entire room shouts in unison. Confetti arcs into the air, shimmering under the fluorescents. A few people blow on noisemakers, hitting an earsplitting note. Harold's caught between fight or flight, scanning the crowd, confused, when he sees me. His shoulders relax and he settles into my favorite expression, the one where his smile strains at his cheekbones and every tooth is visible. He crosses the room, brushing confetti off his head. "What are you doing?" He can't keep himself from smiling. "What is this? Is there an igloo somewhere?"

It's the first time he's mentioned the igloo—our igloo—since June. A bittersweet turn of the knife. I shake it off. "Not this time." The cheering subsides, leaving a ringing in my ears. I fight to stay calm while all the attention settles on us. Raising my voice to carry across the room, I dive in: "Harold. We are all gathered here because we wanted the chance to say thank you. Thank you for all the work you do for basically every club that exists at Belfry. And thank you for what you've done, starting the Pride Club. That was long overdue, but the club couldn't have a better founder."

More cheers, a couple whoops, and scattered applause. Adrenaline courses through me. With a breath I move on to the real point of the surprise party: "And I wanted to get the chance to tell you that I figured out your secret." Harold's face falters. I unfurl the posterboard and hold it up. "I want you to know that I love you just the way you are."

Someone breathes in through a noisemaker, filling the room with a strangled wheeze. Behind Harold, Sasha's cool demeanor falters. Jaws drop all around her. Noisemakers fall limp. The last of the confetti falls in slow motion, silent as snowflakes.

Harold reads the poster and his smile falls.

A few whispers are as audible as shouts:

"Wow, that was Harold?"

"You're gay, man? That's cool! I didn't know!"

Silence falls, and grows more awkward every moment. Harold is dumbstruck. After what feels like a lifetime, he steps forward, so close I have to crane my neck to look up at him. "Ivy, who told you I was gay?"

"I told you, I figured it out! The Pride Club, and the op-ed you wrote? And the . . ." I lean in even more and whisper, "The

igloo? You never even brought it up again. I just thought . . .
Maybe it wasn't . . ."

He shakes his head. His brown eyes grow dark and distant.
He's shutting down—the same look he gets when I decline his
requests to join a club, or that one time I got frustrated and told
him, "It isn't that I don't *understand* Sylow's theorem—it's that
I don't *care*." He got on his bike, went home, and didn't return
my texts for three days.

But worse. This look is so, so much worse.

"I'm not gay," Harold says. Speaking louder, he clarifies to
the room: "I wouldn't have a problem telling you if I was,
because it's nothing to be ashamed of. The only secret I have is
that I . . ." He blinks, considering whether to continue. Staring
daggers right into my soul, he says in a rush: "I'm in love with
you."

I gasp.

This was a moment I played over and over in my mind this
summer. The dream so precious, I barely let myself think it: that
Harold would come back from camp and tell me he realized I
was the one for him. That his feelings were as intense as mine.

That he loved me. As his best friend, and as much, much
more.

I didn't picture it like this. With Sasha looking on, gawking.
With Harold's friends physically leaning in to be closer. In the
back, Heather Schusterman raises her phone, snapping a picture
of this nuclear fallout.

"Harold . . ."

Whispering again, he says: "Didn't you notice the ivy pictures on VEIL? I was trying to tell you. In my own way."

I feel like a bucket of ice has been dropped on my head and it's trickling down my body. The realizations come in phases:

1) I was wrong.

2) Harold isn't gay. Which he just had to clarify, in front of everyone he knows at Belfry.

3) And he just said HE IS *IN LOVE* WITH ME.

The expression on his face right now doesn't say *love*. It says I've shrunk to the size of a pea in his mind. Harold only looks at climate science deniers with this level of disdain.

"You couldn't have just asked?"

I take a step back, flinching. "I—I just . . ."

4) The moment I waited for all summer is here. And I completely ruined it by making a wild assumption, and not just talking to my best friend.

Raising a hand, Harold stops my stammering cold. "You know what? I don't want to hear it." Turning to the room, he shifts into Speech and Debate mode. "I cannot say enough how much I appreciate everyone here. Thank you for the decorations, and the snacks, and Greg, thanks for the noisemakers." He looks around, pointedly avoiding my stare. "This was a great surprise."

Without a backward glance, Harold marches out the door.

The spell that froze me in place breaks when the door slams behind him. I rush to the exit, but Sasha steps in my way.

"That was an extreme miscalculation."

"You have no idea," I snap, shoving past her. No one else dares get between me and the door, but once I'm in the corridor, Harold's already about to turn the corner.

"Harold!" My voice breaks.

Without looking back, he raises a hand in the air and says, loud and firm, "DON'T FOLLOW ME."

The bucket of ice has worked its way all down my body. My hands shake. I feel like my legs might forget how to work at any moment. I'd take vomiting and passing out over this, eight days a week. The door opens again and I'm given the unpleasant realization that things can always get worse.

It's Nate. He's red from his neck to his ears. I've never seen him look this way before—this must be how it feels to get between him and the end zone.

"What was that?" There's none of his usually gentle cadence in the accusation. None of the jokey lightness that makes me look forward to art every day. None of the he's-mad-now-but-won't-be-tomorrow. "What the *hell* was that?"

I shake my head, voice trembling. "I thought . . ."

"It doesn't matter what you thought." Nate has veins in his forehead and his neck. I've never noticed them before. He grabs the posterboard, still rolled in my hand. "You thought Harold wrote those poems?"

"Yeah . . ." I falter. "I thought maybe. Him or someone like him."

"Remember when I warned you about making assumptions about VEIL users?"

I get that feeling like right after the roller coaster cranks into action. Deep, acidic regret.

Voice lowered, he says, "Did it ever occur to you that whoever wrote those poems had a *reason* for keeping them on an anonymous site? That maybe it isn't okay to try to figure out who they are, and that it *definitely* isn't okay to try to tell the world that someone is gay without their permission?"

His voice raises to a shout in spite of himself. He turns away from me, covering his face with my drawing. "Me," Nate says in a husky breath. "The person who posts these poems to VEIL? It's me." He looks around, anger giving way to paranoia.

The icy shock has started to wear off. I'm beginning to connect the dots:

1) Nate is gay.

2) Tag is Nate's brother.

3) Nate doesn't feel like he can come out.

4) Nate has been living in a confusing personal hell.

5) I've misread everything.

"But the Pride Club," I say, floundering. "It's a safe place!"

Nate shakes his head, his gaze steely. "Stuff always gets out. Because of people like you."

My insides feel like they're collapsing into a black hole. Only I'm not actually that lucky—if I was going supernova, I could escape this reality, where I was so, so wrong about how to be there for people I love.

"Nate—" I take a step toward him.

He holds a hand out to protect the distance between us. "Don't," he says. "Don't use your friend voice with me. We are not friends right now. We aren't friends anymore." He rolls up the drawing and shoves it at me. "Forget Burmkezerg. You're worse."

I clutch the painting and hold it to my chest like a shield. Nate storms past me. And, like Harold before him, he takes the turn at the end of the hall without a backward glance.

The two people I felt closest to are racing to get as far away from me as possible. And it's entirely my fault.

The door slams open and Sasha strides out. She crosses her arms.

I bristle.

Sasha considers me. "For what it's worth, I like your drawing."

"It's a collage," I mutter.

"If I were you, I'd burn it." Sasha returns to the room filled with people, all of them more thoughtful, kinder, and more mature than me. Every one of them better suited to be Harold's friends, or his girlfriend.

But it turns out he'd loved *me*.

And I've ruined it. For good.

B est friends, or friends of any stripe—
E ager to help, unwilling to learn—
T ake their toll.
R are, it seems, are those who,
A ware of their limits,
Y ield to the rights of others.
A ll I wanted was a little
L oyalty.

To: msianmalcolm@geemail.com
From: tha_burm@veil.yolo
Subject: Buh Bye

Dear VEIL Users,

Hey. Rake here. I'm writing this letter without Legal. Without the board. Without an office full of "brand consultants" and PR flaks trying to tell me how to run my business. I fired them all.

Actually, that's a little misleading. I didn't fire anyone—technically, I quit. But I did one last thing at my desk. While the board was already on the phone with every floating CEO and bloodthirsty VC in Silicon Valley, I did the only thing I still could.

I deleted VEIL.

It's gone. All the art, all the pictures, all the poems, all the videos. Gone.

For years, I reminded everyone of the mission: to embrace the temporary. To open up to the honesty of anonymous, spontaneous moments—for better or for worse. What did people do instead? Worked to crack the anonymous algorithm, trying to get their face in the frame; got mad when a post was allegedly about them; sued me and my company when people got ugly.

I have news for you. People *are* ugly. But they're kind, generous, and loving, too.

And then they're gone.

So, as my final act as founder, CEO, and all-around head honcho of VEIL, I leave you with the memories of all the beautiful, meaningful, awful, offensive, and thought-provoking work that kept you coming back to VEIL. Just the memories. And the knowledge that all of that, like life, was temporary.

One love,
Rake

CHAPTER 27

I remember when I thought the first day of tenth grade was hard because I had to get through it without Harold.

Ha.

I wish Today Ivy could go back in time and show First-Day Ivy this scene: walking across campus in the middle of the semester and not being able to look *anyone* in the eye. In a sick way, I'm envious of Tag. Being expelled means Tag sits in his room worrying that everyone might hate him. I get to know for sure.

No one who knows Harold will talk to me. No one who cares about gay rights will talk to me. Nate won't talk to me. There's a pretty big overlap in that Venn diagram. Like . . . the entire school.

One thing becomes painfully clear, and fast: There's a big difference between being socially averse and actually being an outcast. Up until this point, not talking to anyone at school was my choice. But PHHM (Post–Huge Harold Mistake), people turn away when I try to so much as ask for a pencil, or burst into tittering laughter when I walk past. *That's* what being a true outcast feels like.

Sadly, not much has changed in how often I see Harold. But there aren't even occasional check-in texts anymore. He cut me off, cold turkey. Nate, on the other hand, is torture. We still share a table whenever art meets in the D wing, and no matter what, there's an hour every day when I feel like I'm taking half breaths, hoping against all logic and reason that he'll show up and say, "I've decided to forgive you."

When Tag's suspension is finally lifted, it gets even worse. Tag's a bit of a pariah, too, and Nate's put in the awkward position of having to eat lunch with him. Watching Nate be a good brother breaks my heart. I know now what he's been hiding all this time, and how much it must cost him to constantly put Tag's best interests over his own. If he were still talking to me, I'd tell him that at some point Tag needs to learn to take his own lumps. But that's a laughably big "if."

It's no better at home, where I've taken to faking illness to avoid the dinner table. I don't even want to think about sitting there while Mom and Dad talk about how VEIL shutting down is "all for the best," and I'll understand when I'm older. Not that they necessarily would have said that, but it's worst-case scenario. Better not to risk it.

So I've taken to spending as much time as possible in the darkroom. Still exploring the double exposure and messing with distorting VEIL images, but the end results are getting darker, literally and figuratively. They give me this kind of sad and familiar feeling. Like when thinking about childhood joys just reminds you of the relentless march of time.

I'm listening to *a lot* of Lana Del Rey.

My plan to avoid reality and turn into a hobbit is going swimmingly until, one day a few weeks after The Incident, I get home to find my father guarding the staircase.

"Ivy Elizabeth Harrison," he says in a stern sitcom-father voice I almost never hear. "We are having a family meeting."

"But I . . ."

"Feel sick? Nice try." He points to the family room, where Mom is sitting with her feet tucked primly beneath her, hands folded in her lap.

They set a trap, the tricky minxes.

I sulk into the room and sink into the chair. "What is this? An intervention?"

"Maybe," Mom says.

"The TV crew's on standby," Dad quips, settling beside her on the couch. Mom shoots him a look. He clears his throat and looks at the ground.

"Ivy, we wanted to have a family meeting to talk to you, because you seem . . ." Mom sighs. "Suboptimal."

Good thing there's no TV crew here. This is some truly amateur intervening.

"Um, yeah. Definitely not great," I say.

Dad looks at me. "Do you want to talk about it? Believe it or not, we grown-up people have some words of wisdom every now and again."

"Wisdom," I huff, crossing my arms. "Like how wise it was to get involved in the VEIL witch hunt and kill your daughter's favorite app?"

Mom holds a hand up. "Let's be careful about the term 'witch hunt.' Rake Burmkezerg is a multimillionaire and VEIL caused demonstrable harm. That doesn't exactly equate with innocent women dying for patriarchal panic."

"Mom!" I whine.

"Let me translate," Dad says. "Veronica, I hear that Ivy is upset with us for contributing to the ultimate demise of something she enjoyed. Ivy, your mother is a scientist and a feminist, and as such believes strongly that words have specific meanings."

What if I could actually make myself throw up? Would that get me out of here?

Dad continues: "We want to clarify some things. You should have all the information first. Then, if you still want to be angry with us, that's your right."

Mom nods. Turning to me, I can see how pale and splotchy her hands are from twisting tightly together. "The truth is, we were getting ready to settle with VEIL. The parents didn't have the resources to pursue a long, drawn-out legal battle, nor did we want to. We only wanted the app to put more constraints in place to protect minors."

"The lawyers were close to figuring things out," Dad says. "Then we started hearing about all the other lawsuits filed against Burmkezerg for similar stuff. Hate speech, trolling, death threats, doxxing—which I had to look up, and it is terrifying. VEIL was getting hit on a lot of different fronts."

"The lawyers assured us that things at VEIL were going to change," Mom says.

"Well, I didn't think Burmkezerg shut down the site *just* cuz of you guys," I grumble. "He had to shut it down before it got turned into something else. Just another social media site."

Mom and Dad look at each other. Gently, Mom says, "It was worse than that, Ivy. The things that VEIL was getting sued over—frankly, we're lucky, in a way. What Tag wrote was terrible, but it wasn't a death threat against anyone specific, and it didn't boil over into action outside of VEIL. Some of the other cases were more extreme. And Burmkezerg didn't want to take responsibility for any of it. He refused to see that the app was causing real-world harm."

And, though of course I knew that VEIL was huge outside of my little Sudden Cove bubble, this is really the first time it occurs to me: Stuff like this must be happening elsewhere. I mean, of course! But being so consumed with the app has sort of shrunk my worldview . . . to whatever's been happening within five miles of me.

Ugh.

"We didn't want to destroy something you loved," Dad says. "But honey—your fave was problematic."

Mom nods gravely. "Word."

I fight so hard against the laugh—seriously, I do—but ultimately I break down. It really, really, really sucks to have funny parents sometimes.

"So, your mother and I were thinking about what it means for you, now that VEIL is gone." Dad looks hesitant.

Mom picks it up: "That's when we realized—we didn't really understand what you were getting out of the app. You said you never posted to VEIL, and I believe you. But we want help understanding why it meant so much to you, and how we can help you find that elsewhere."

Under their twin stares, I will myself to get swallowed whole by the armchair. "I don't know," I mumble.

Mom shakes her head. "Gotta do better than that, babe."

"Well, there was just, like, a ton of great art on there." I pick at the upholstery.

"Mmm-hmmm." They keep staring.

"It was like people on there *got it*," I say, ducking my head. "They saw the world the same way I do. Most of them, anyway." I think of all the pictures I've developed, all the new works I've built from the collective VEIL creativity. "They made me want to be a better artist. And they made me feel . . ." I take a deep breath. "Made me feel like maybe someday I could be a serious artist, too."

I raise my eyes just in time to see Mom and Dad exchange a confused look.

"Someday?" Dad asks, surprised.

"You've taken hundreds, probably thousands, of photographs." Mom holds her hand out toward the hallway. "Your art is already framed in our house."

"Do you mean the pictures of *you*? Framed in the entryway?" My tone is biting. "The only pictures of mine framed in this whole house and they're just shots of you guys doing your jobs. Saving the world and stuff, being way more important than an amateur photographer could ever hope to be."

"What?" Dad sits straight up, all his usual humor stripped away. "Is *that* why you think we framed your project?" He stands. "Come here and look at it with me again. Right now."

Reluctantly, I follow Dad into the front hallway. Arms crossed, I take in the set of photographs I've stared at, coming and going, for years. They're from one long day when I accompanied my parents and a series of volunteers to tide pools at the mouth of the San Lorenzo River. They were collecting samples to show how deforestation was clogging rivers and natural wells with silt and junk. One entire Saturday spent hiking along a river, from mountaintop to ocean delta, with me snapping pictures throughout.

Since we were out all day long, I had the chance to consider my photographs in a way I hadn't before. Up to that point, I'd mostly been doing point-and-shoot pictures of my feet in sand, or of clouds over the ocean. That day, I had time to prep for the moment that Mom would dip her hand in the crystal-blue river and come up with a vial of water shot through with settling sediment. The way Mom looked at the sample was almost romantic. Light danced through the vial's uneven prism, making it seem like she held liquid silver. I had time to find the best angle to capture the hourly group check-in. Dad wore a case around his neck like a hot-dog vendor at a ballpark. It was meant to hold vials, and volunteers swarmed him to get their samples properly labeled and stored. In the photo, he's visibly elated by the chaos.

"I'll never forget when we went to have your rolls of film developed, seeing them for the first time. I don't know how much you'll understand this feeling, but . . ." Dad shakes his head, smiling at the project. "It was the first time I really got to see what you see. How you framed the pictures, and the way you noticed the light. It gave me a sense of how you see your mother and me, and also how you see the world. It was, and is, incredibly special."

Dad wipes his mouth and blinks.

"You've always been a real artist," Mom says. "*That's* why we framed these pictures."

Shiny-eyed, Dad pulls me into a huge hug. Mom piles on. I don't know what to say. The pictures look different to me now, knowing how my parents see them: as moments from their lives, captured by their daughter, used to discuss the importance of their life's work.

"We would gladly frame more of your work, but you started piling the pictures in your room," Mom says. "We thought maybe you had a system? Or that you didn't want anyone to look at them. In hindsight, I wish I had asked more questions, but I wanted to respect your privacy."

Dad perks up. "Oh, do we not have to pretend to do that anymore?"

Mom punches him lightly in the arm.

I give another huff of a laugh. The laugh builds, then morphs, and then I'm crying. Mom and Dad step in to hug me again. They guide me to the couch and sit me down between them.

"Something tells me this isn't all about Rake Burmkezerg," Mom says.

I shake my head.

"Do you want to talk about it?"

I shake my head again.

Dad squeezes my shoulder. "One thing at a time," he says. "Just know we're always here for you. We love you."

I drag my snotty self upstairs and collapse in the chair at my desk. I fire up the computer, ready to lose myself in scrolling through RogueArtiste. It's no VEIL, but I've been finding some pretty cool stuff. And I have to admit there's something nice about art with attribution.

A buzz tells me I have a new email.

To: msianmalcolm@geemail.com
From: tha_burm@veil.yolo
Subject: Srsly

Dear VEIL Users,

Hey. Rake here. We meet again. Ha.

In the weeks since I deleted VEIL, it seems like everything has blown up. I'm getting sued by the company I founded, and I'm still named in two-dozen-odd outstanding lawsuits. Thousands of you have flooded my social media to let me know just how much of a slime-swallowing cretin I am for deleting an app. Some stuff has shown up at my house—I've hired security.

I've got news for you people: VEIL is just an app. It disappearing from your phone isn't exactly the fall of Rome. If losing it left that big a hole in your life, you might want to examine your choices.

But, hey. I created VEIL because I wanted to inspire people to share their art and themselves. I'm glad so many of you loved it. And I'm sorry you're so upset that it's gone now. But the power to create and share that art has always existed for you. Go elsewhere on the internet. Go to an art gallery. Take a class. Get out there and express yourself. You never needed me to do that.

Now that you got the chance with VEIL, maybe you'll get brave enough to do it elsewhere. In the meantime, stop showing up at my mom's church, okay?

One love,

Rake

Well, it's official: Rake Burmkezerg is a twaddling dillhole.

I shut the computer and stare out the window. Between VEIL and Goldblum mania and my painting jags, it seems like forever since I sat at my desk and watched the salt air gently bend the palm trees. My window faces Harold's house. Just a few blocks away, my former best friend who at some point loved me is . . . doing what? Sleeping in his car in the garage, still? Or maybe he's also sitting on his bed, looking out his window, watching the sunset paint the rooftops between us a candied shade of pink.

And Nate? I never even got the chance to see Nate's house, or his room. I don't know what direction he's facing, or the state of his heart.

But reading through Burmkezerg's pathetic letter once more, something becomes overwhelmingly clear.

It's time for me to own up to my own stuff.

While Rake Burmkezerg, known twaddling dillhole, may have many faults, he is right about one thing: I do not now—nor have I ever—needed him or VEIL to share my art. It only felt like I did. Now I understand that, where people like Nate used VEIL's anonymity as a shelter from harm, I'd clung to it as a scapegoat to avoid standing behind my work. It felt like I'd been waiting for some sign to let me know it was time to be taken seriously. Like something was going to reassure me that no one would ever criticize my art.

But then I think about Ajeet feeling brave enough to talk about his cancer diagnosis. Or Loretta getting the courage to turn in artwork that dealt with her parents' divorce. Or Jaz accepting the lead in the musical. Once I told them that I knew who they were on VEIL, they dared to bring their genius—and their pain—into the real world.

Truth is, someone's always going to be ready to criticize my art. Anyone's art. Some people have nothing better to do than tear others down for trying. We can't let that keep us from taking chances. Because I love my work and it makes me happy. And now I know that Mom and Dad love it, too.

That's enough. It has to be.

I open a new browser window and click to the search bar: ART+SUMMER+CAMP+PHOTOGRAPHY.

Here goes nothing.

CHAPTER 28

The other thing I realized from reading Burmkezerg's Pettysburg Address: It's time to own up to my mistakes. Starting with Nate, and Harold, and Jaz. It doesn't matter what my intentions were; my actions hurt people. And unlike Burmkezerg, I know that saying "I'm sorry you're upset" doesn't count as a real apology.

It's on me to set this right. Even if Harold, Nate, and Jaz don't forgive me, I have to try.

It's all on me.

Turns out that is *much* easier said than done.

I try to take up as little space as possible in the packed hallway by Jaz Clarke's locker. My heart bangs against my chest. I'm so nervous I feel like I'm about to vibrate out of my own skin. My nails are bitten to nubs and my eyes are puffy and red. I stayed awake all night thinking of every possible way to apologize.

And, as Jaz approaches, they all fly right out of my head.

"Hey," she greets me dully, opening her locker door to block my face.

I bite my lip and step out from behind the door. "I just wanted to say one thing."

"If it's sorry, you can stuff your sorrys in a basket."

I take a breath. "It *is* sorry. Jaz, I am so, so, so sorry."

She swaps out an anthology of English Romantic poets for an econ book, but I can tell she's working through something in her mind.

I jump into the silence, unable to bear it any longer. "I just know you have such an amazing voice. And how much you love musicals. And . . . I thought I was doing something nice, but now I understand: There's a difference between being supportive and being interventionist. And I crossed the line."

The silence lapses between us again. Jaz snaps her backpack shut and slams the locker, spinning its combo lock.

"That really sucked," she says, staring right into my eyes. Her lips, usually tilted like she's in on a joke, are set in a deadly serious line. Her dark eyes bore into mine. "You had no right to sign me up without my knowledge or consent."

I nod furiously. "You're right. I'm so sorry."

Jaz pauses. Her lips scrunch a bit; her eyes crinkle at the corners. "Did you see Vivienne Hansen's face, though? When I hit that note?"

My eyebrows wiggle. "Did I ever."

"She nearly crapped herself."

"Well, good thing the star of the show doesn't have to clean up that kind of mess."

Jaz throws her head back and laughs. I take my first solid breath in over a minute.

"Ugh, Ivy, I know you meant well, but you seriously almost sent me to an early grave," Jaz says, starting to walk toward her class. "Are you going this way?"

I nod, even though my third-period class is in the opposite direction. "I'm learning something about that feeling," I tell her.

"The early grave?"

"Yeah. I think I buried myself alive."

Jaz sighs sympathetically. "I heard about Harold and the party. You're on a roll."

I cover my face, groaning.

"It's gonna take a lot more than hanging outside Harold's locker to make up for that one," Jaz says, leaning on a classroom door. "But hey—if you need help, let me know."

I pause. "Thank you."

Jaz ducks into class just as the bell rings.

The relief from our conversation doesn't last long. In art I sit beside Nate and hold my breath the entire time. It's like I'm waiting for some kind of sign that he's open to hearing what I have to say. Not surprisingly, no sign ever comes. That's the thing about big life moments: They don't announce themselves. Change is just a matter of making up your mind and following through, over and over again. The making-up-your-mind part is a real doozy, though.

The bell rings and I haven't come any closer to apologizing to Nate. We've only shared fleeting eye contact, which leaves us both flushed and tense.

After school, I march through the cafeteria to the art dome. The darkroom has become my oasis. The room is always the same: dark. The process is always the same: exposure, development bath, stop bath, rinse, hang, admire. It feels like the only thing that's the same as before.

Throwing open the dome's creaky door, I stop just over the threshold, frozen. The door to the darkroom—the tiny closet space that, as far as I can tell, only I have ever used—is wide open. The dome door slams into my butt and I leap forward with a squeal as it shuts, throwing the dome into almost total darkness. The only light is from the skylights, and the soft red glow from the darkroom's single bulb.

A figure appears in the shadows. My heart leaps into my throat.

With a flick, the figure switches on the dome's lights. It's Ms. H.

I exhale noisily, bending over to rest my hands on my knees.

"Sorry!" Ms. H says, laughing. "I see how this could be a little creepy."

"A little," I say, clutching my heart.

"I was hoping you'd come to studio time today," Ms. H says. "I need to talk to you about something." She motions for me to follow her into the darkroom.

The far wall is lined with rungs of string to hang drying prints. Every rung has been filled with photos, clipped to the string with clothespins. Every single print hanging on the wall is one I've developed over the last couple of weeks—all my double- and triple-exposure experiments, based on VEIL posts.

My heart leaps into my throat.

This is it: the moment I've dreaded. The moment Ms. H sees that I'm a fraud, incapable of coming up with my own original work. That I'm consumed with thinking about other people's art and can't seem to branch out on my own. That she was wrong to build me a darkroom and give me all this time to use it for derivative hackery.

"These are all yours, yes?" she asks.

Obviously they are all mine. There's a similarity to them all—a collective sadness. Seeing them all together, it looks as obvious to me as the paint splatter theme in a series of Jackson Pollocks.

"Um. Yes." There's no point in lying.

Ms. H looks from the prints, to me, and back. "Why haven't I seen these before? Why aren't you turning them in as your assignments?"

Where to begin? It isn't entirely my work? I'm stealing?

"Those aren't all my images," I say. "I took pictures of some of my favorite VEIL posts. There were so many images on VEIL I couldn't let go of. So I took pictures of them and then layered my own work over them." I'm surprised by the tears that spring to my eyes. With Ms. H staring at me, I can only think of how much I miss the constant creativity and inspiration of VEIL. I miss it like a friend who moved away, or a favorite show that was canceled. It's never coming back and there's a kind of grief to that, though I hate even admitting it to myself. It seems so trivial. But it wasn't, not to me.

"So," Ms. H says, drawing the word out. She shuffles between the pictures, holding them up to compare against the hanging prints. "You didn't show these to me because they were based on other people's work. And you thought that was cheating."

"That *is* cheating," I correct her.

Ms. H laughs to herself. "Ivy. You're so pure."

I frown. Is that a compliment?

She looks at me, a smile teasing the corners of her lips. "It's fine to be influenced by the works of others. Yes, the way you've incorporated others' works is a bit literal. But you haven't reproduced anyone's work in its original form. All of these prints are you taking a VEIL post and transmogrifying it into something new, something original. Something completely your own."

Ms. H walks over to the wall of prints and takes one down. It's the one with the upside-down balanced rocks. She holds it up so we can both observe. "This—see? It doesn't matter which of the images you have here is yours. You've manipulated them in such a way that they are something new entirely." Ms. H considers the print. "This is original. It has a point of view. It's an expression."

It feels like Ms. H is giving me a Get Out of Jail Free card. The explanation is too easy, too convenient. "I stole those images," I protest. "This work isn't really mine."

She considers me. Pointing to the wall, she asks: "Do you see the connective tissue of all these images?"

I hesitate until it's clear that this isn't a rhetorical question. "They're . . ." I stare at the combined force of all my prints. They're all a shade too dark. They're all something like my skin turned inside out. "They're sad."

"They have a melancholy, yes," Ms. H says, nodding. "They have a consistency. Of color tones, of composition, of tenor. They are a collection."

I tilt my head, considering my own work.

"This work is more than worthy of the student showcase," Ms. H says, her voice low, a whisper, even though it's only the two of us in this expansive dome. "This is the work I knew to expect from you."

I've spent so much of the last few weeks focusing only on my mistakes. The compliment washes over me, slowly. Tears roll down my cheeks. I duck my head so hair hides the emotional outburst from Ms. H.

She sees it anyway.

Wrapping an arm around my shoulders, Ms. H squeezes tight. "Seems like you're going through something. That's okay.

The only way to get through awful times is to art. Art as hard as you can."

"So I'm in the showcase?" I ask, wiping my eyes. As the compliment settles in, so, too, do the possibilities. The seedling of a plan has nestled in my mind, and with it a long-forgotten sense of hope.

Ms. H nods, dropping her arm. "Yes, as long as you promise not to keep work like this from me anymore."

A smile breaks across my face like sunlight breaking through a cloud. "Ms. H, I have an idea. Do you think you could help me with something?"

"Anything, kiddo."

I take a breath.

And then I tell her everything.

CHAPTER 29

By the time the last bell rings on the day of the art dome gallery opening, my plan's already afoot. I make my way to my locker, ambling slowly and watching the time tick away on my watch. By now, Harold will be checking his voice mail, where Patton will inform him that his roll of film at Aperture Rapture has been developed and is ready to be picked up. Harold has this thing about voice mails—he actually checks them. And he's so diligent, he once went to an eye doctor appointment that was actually meant for ANOTHER Harold Johnson, just because he can't say no to an automated appointment reminder. With that in mind, I'd asked Patton to do his best imitation of a robot voice, which I can only imagine led to Harold listening to the creepiest message ever.

Anyhow, by now he should be at Aperture Rapture, befuddled by the envelope of images that Patton slides across the counter to him, free of charge. Harold will flip through the shots: me holding up the board game Sorry! and looking pathetic. A close-up of a calculator readout that says 50887 (that's "sorry" in the calculator code Harold taught me last year, when we had Algebra 1 together). And then a series where I wrote out, on a whiteboard, "I'm sorry, Harold. Can you ever forgive me?" with boxes next to the words "Yes," "No," and "Maybe." "If either Yes or Maybe, proceed to Beach Reads."

I close my locker and mosey on over to Leibovitz. On my leisurely bike ride home, I imagine where Harold is now: at Beach Reads, where Kristi waits for him with his second gift. Jaz was excited when I took her up on her offer to help. I filled her in on the logistics of the whole plan and, working together, we made a custom treasure map. The first X marking the spot is at the bookstore. Beside it I wrote, "Harold. I've missed you. This year you've been as hard to find as the mythical grouches in this mysterious hunting ground."

I lean Leibovitz on the front porch and burst inside. I throw my school stuff on the bed and make a Superman-quick transformation into after-school Ivy. She wears all black, like daytime Ivy, but her dress has a little shimmer to it, her bun gets swept up with a glittery black bow, and her tights have little spiderwebs all over them—Harold's favorite.

All bedecked in my nighttime apparel, I grab a little leather backpack and hop right back on Leibovitz. I gotta book it to the school to head off Harold, who is no doubt still wandering through Elbow's Temple.

In what some might actually consider a religious miracle, I managed to find a descendant of Elbow himself. Turns out, my parents know a lot of people, and the people they know know people, and on and on until you get to the fact that Elbow's family still lives in nearby Scotts Valley. His granddaughter Adelaide seems quite nice, and said my request tickled her as she hasn't been tickled in ages. It's going to completely and utterly blow Harold's mind.

With the family's permission, I planted a gaggle of new gnomes, each one bearing part of a full letter I wrote to Harold.

(1/5) Dear Harold: First of all, I'm a jerk. I just want to get that out of the way right now. The jerk store is closed cuz they ran out of me.

(2/5) When I built you that birthday igloo, a part of me hoped we would crawl in separately and emerge together. I still think about the look on your face as you lay on that grassy blanket and looked up at the fauxrealis.

(3/5) I should have been more helpful when you came back from camp. You've always helped me when I was overwhelmed, or scared, or not sure what to do. Thinking of how alone you must have felt then makes me want to cry.

(4/5) You've been so busy this year. And instead of working hard to make time with you, I withdrew. I felt rejected, and I was scared. You deserved better from the person who claims to be your best friend.

(5/5) I wanted an explanation for something so badly, I twisted the truth beyond recognition. Kind of how my favorite cryptozoological historian keeps working on his theories to suit the moment. The beast itself (or at least the version of it that guards the door) holds the next clue.

Once Harold gathers all the gnomes and sends them into the chute of mystery, his prize will be the final part of the letter, with its clue.

I didn't have the brass boobs to ask the Bigfoot Museum curator to give Harold a clue personally. To be honest, I didn't have the time. There's no way to walk into that place without getting a forty-minute explanation of how Pangaea makes the existence of Bigfoot practically a foregone conclusion.

So instead I wrote the final clue on a piece of paper, curled it up, and tucked it in the mouth of the giant Bigfoot statue that stands by the museum's front door. Harold will find it no prob-lem. That'll have him driving back to the school, where it all started.

Where I'm headed now.

The school at dusk is eerily silent. Chimichanga wrappers blow across the halls like tumbleweeds. The sound of distant conver-sations carry across the quad.

So far I haven't heard the thing I'm really listening for: Jaz and the Belfry Basstones singing an a cappella rendition of "The Way You Make Me Feel." Harold will hate having people sing his favorite song to him, but a little embarrassment does a body good. Besides, it's a part of the spectacle of the thing. What's a grand gesture without a serenade?

When she has Harold cringing, Jaz will hand him the final note:

Check the darkroom.

The door to the darkroom has been decorated with a heart, and once he walks inside, Harold will be surrounded by pictures that remind me of him. The shots of him in front of his news wall, candids I took at lunch last year when he thought I was experimenting with my aperture settings. And, biggest of all, a print of that moment in the igloo. Of our feet, gently leaning together, in a moment when we almost said everything we wanted to but were too scared.

That's when I want to be waiting outside, to see his expression. And ask if he's up for giving me another chance.

Groups are making their way to the back lot of Belfry, where the gallery opening is about to officially begin. The sun has set. The sky is a blend of plums, indigos, and navy blues. The ponderosa pines and palmettos cut Seussian figures in the night. Distant conversation wafts through the otherwise silent Z wing.

My fears begin to boil under the surface. That Harold never even started the scavenger hunt. That he doesn't care about what we've been to each other. That I really and truly ruined the best thing I ever had.

I shake my head, scared to let myself wander too far down that path. But it echoes in the back of my mind as I get closer and closer without hearing the Basstones' dulcet tones.

The buzz of crowd noise spills out into the night from the art dome's open door. Interior light shines through the sky-lights and casts a long triangle of warm light across the dark asphalt of the Z wing. People actually showed up for the show-case! Probably lured by the invite's promise of free cheese and crackers.

When I get to the gallery door, the Basstones are nowhere to be found. The slivers in my heart turn to cracks. I wander around the back, and to the theater, returning to the front door. Not so much as a pitch pipe in sight.

My heart sinks down to my shoes. So that's it, then. All of it, all my hard work, the great grand gesture, was for nothing. The damage I'd already done was too great for Harold to forgive.

Footsteps crunch behind me.

Nate. He looks resigned.

It's Nate—and Tag.

I've never actually spoken to Tag before, or been this close. Though they're identical twins, the difference between Nate and Tag is blazingly clear to me. Tag has the hunched, wary look of someone waiting for an attack. That couldn't be more different from Nate's usual confident saunter—though today Nate approaches with halting steps. My heart lurches with the desire to reach out and hug him, or squeeze his arm, or something. Anything. To regain his trust in an instant.

But I know that isn't possible. I settle for a nervous smile.

"Hey," I say.

"Hi," Nate says. His smile is the same one he flashed at the Bigfoot Museum after the curator suggested interdimensional time travel. After getting the chance to know Nate's *real* smile, this fake one is a sad copy.

Tag does a half-salute thing. "I'm Tag."

"I know." I steel myself and launch into it. "Listen—if you never want to talk to me again, that is okay. But I just want to say . . ." I stop short. Nervously, I look at Tag. I realize I have no idea whether Nate has come out to his brother.

Nate puts his hands in his pockets. "He knows."

"Yep." Tag looks between us. "I know."

Nate looks at his brother. "And we're working on it."

That lightens my heart, at least a bit. "Well then. I wanted to say that I've never felt worse about anything in my entire life. Trying to out someone—that was so, so wrong. And if I had gotten it right—if I had figured out it was you . . ." I glance around quickly, quadruple-checking that we are the only ones listening in to this conversation. "I can't believe I was so thought-less. And I never will be again. That I promise you."

Nate stares at our feet. I wiggle my pigeon toes.

"I want to earn your trust back, more than anything," I say. "I miss my friend." I feel the sharp sting of tears welling. Tag's gaze sits on me like a weight.

When Nate meets my eyes, there's not even a tiny shred of humor in his expression. "Well, you and Tag are the only ones who know. So for starters you can keep my secret."

With a sweep of the hand, I mime locking my mouth and throwing away the key.

That wins me an itty-bitty grin. I'll take it.

"As for being friends again—let's take it day by day." Nate looks over his shoulder, back toward the studio. "Have fun in there," he says mysteriously. Nodding to Tag, Nate spins and starts walking away.

Tag hesitates. He steps nearer to me, looming over my head. "Hey—I was meaning to find you at school sometime to say this, but . . . I wanted to say thank you."

I tilt my head, confused.

Tag glances back at Nate, who has paused. Quickly, he says, "Thank you for being there for Nate. When I wasn't."

The two walk away together, into the growing dark.

My skin is covered in goose bumps. I make fists to keep my hands from shaking. For a minute, I thought I might be in love with Nate Gehrig, but now I know the truth: He's one of the best, most interesting, most fun people I've ever met. And I want desperately to get out of my own way and earn my right to go back to being buds.

Well. That leaves one thing: the showcase.

Inside, parents and students meander, holding plastic flutes filled with fizzing apple cider, munching on cheese, crackers, and fragrant jalapeño crab cakes. In the center of the room is a huge robot statue made up of rocks, seaweed, and warped wood that looks like it was washed up on shore.

The right-hand wall is covered with art I recognize from Loretta, her series of dollhouse scenes. She even brought in the actual dollhouse so people could compare the real thing to how she represented its rooms and angles in her photos. I feel a swell of pride seeing how gorgeous all the work looks when presented together.

I turn to take in the other half of the gallery and pull up short. I helped Ms. H frame all my prints, but she insisted on putting them up herself. Now I see why. The prints are all black and white, and the frames are IKEA brown/black. But they've been hung on the wall in the shape of a heart.

"If you see a faded sign by the side of the road . . ."

I spin in place. Jaz smiles at me. She's flanked by the Basstones, all wearing tuxedo T-shirts. They belt out a slo-jam rendition of "Love Shack."

Adrenaline pumps through me. There's only one person who knows how much I love that song.

Turning back toward my photos, I pick out Ms. H, my parents, Heather, Patton, and Kristi among the crowd of people gathered. They're almost too happy, too eager. Then their eyes shift to something over my shoulder.

The darkroom door.

It opens and a figure in a suit steps out from the crowd.

It's Harold.

He's wearing a suit, with a gray checked shirt, and a red Steve Zissou beanie that matches his red Air Maxes. He looks incredible.

He got a haircut is my first thought, because I am ridiculous.

My second thought isn't a thought so much as a compulsion: I launch myself at him, throwing my whole self into a hug. And, to my intense, profound relief, Harold hugs me right back.

"I thought you gave up on me," I say, my voice muffled into his shoulder.

Harold squeezes me tighter. "Nah. I was just one step ahead of you this time."

I lean back. "Ms. H?"

"Called me out of ASB and broke it all down for me. Helped arrange everything."

Well, well, well. "The student has become the teacher."

Harold looks extremely proud of himself. "I learned from the best." Releasing my hands, he looks over at the wall of photographs and back to me. "I couldn't miss this. You finally showed someone your art."

I pull back, rocking back on my heels. "Yep. I had this really smart friend who tried to convince me to do that a long time ago, but I could never work up the nerve. I thought now was the time to listen to him for a change."

Grabbing Harold's hands, I fight to keep my voice even. "I'm sorry." I've said it a bunch—in unanswered texts and emails, in a note tied to a car wash voucher I left on his wind-shield, and in Morse code dots and lines that I slipped into his locker almost every day. But I think I'm more likely to regret the apologies I don't give. "And there's something else."

Harold raises an eyebrow.

"I want to join Pride Club. And Key Club. And 4-H. I want to join any club that'll have me. I'm ready."

Harold grins, looking slightly pained. His gaze rolls over my face, my hair, my dress. "Funny. I was thinking of taking a few off my plate." Meeting my eyes again, he adds: "Someone gave me really good advice. Turns out it's possible to say no? Anyway, I think I need to see my friends more. They tend to go off the deep end without me."

Staring up at Harold's dark, misty eyes, I'm filled with some-thing so pleasant I don't have a more accurate way of describing it than *sure*. Like I've stumbled on something completely true, a proven scientific theory. It feels good to have something so *known* before me.

"Remember when you said you loved me?" I whisper.

Harold nods. "Yes. It's your turn."

Forget that. Raising up to my tiptoes, I throw my arms around Harold's neck and pull him in for a kiss. It's light and sweet, and we can't stop smiling, and people start to cheer. The most incredible random act of kindness I could have ever received.

It's pure art.

ACKNOWLEDGMENTS

I've been waiting ten years to write this page. I'm going to spill a lot of ink.

Thank you to Amanda Maciel, for being such an insightful and patient editor and for sharing so much of yourself during the crafting of this book. To David Levithan, who has no idea how much it meant when he complimented my first pages at ALA. To Talia Seidenfeld, for her thoughtful reads and behind-the-scenes encouragement. To Melissa Schirmer and Jacqueline Hornberger for caring about yetis and Teen Beat eyes. To Nina Goffi for designing the book, Michael Frost for his photography, and Chris Stengel for pulling everything together.

To Sarah Burnes, for believing in me for so long and sticking with me through so much. Not every agent would sit with their new client while she cried on the floor of the Javits Center. Your unwavering faith has made all the difference. And to Logan Garrison Savits for all your kind words and guidance.

To Miranda Popkey, for your Santa Cruz perspective.

To Kirsten Hubbard and Maurene Goo, my author spouses and cheerleaders and most important sounding boards. And all the young adult authors who make up the wonderful Los Angeles KidLit community, especially Victoria Aveyard, Anna Carey, Brandy Colbert, Marie Lu, Tahereh Mafi, Morgan Matson, Zan Romanoff, Aminah Mae Safi, and Elissa Sussman. To Margaret Stohl, who opened so many doors and even some windows for me.

Speaking of Los Angeles: to the owners and staff of Dinosaur, the Semi-Tropic, and Bon Vivant. Without your welcoming spirits (and strong drinks), this book wouldn't have been written. Or the next one. Or the one after that. Thanks for putting the shingle out for bums like me who sit too long, crying at screens or staring into space.

To Arcade Fire for "Everything Now" and DJDS for "Trees on Fire," the songs that got me through the draft that mattered.

To all the women who made up YA Highway, especially Kate Hart, Kaitlin Ward, Somaiya Daud, Michelle Schusterman, Stephanie Kuehn, and Amy Lukavics. To the hags, especially Lindsay Roth Culli, Kara Thomas, Samantha Mabry, Courtney Summers, Laurie Devore. And to Veronica Roth, who has been both and more: I love exploring worlds, fictional and otherwise, with you.

To every single writer who has made time for the First Draft podcast, and for all the show's incredibly supportive listeners: thank you. The KidLit community transformed my life and filled it with passion, understanding, and joy.

To Megan O'Connor and Danielle McLaughlin, without whom I never would have survived my own adolescence and who have shaped everything I am as a person and a friend. Shadows of their love are on every page.

To the Andersons, the Seebergers, the Bryants, and the Warners: I have no idea how to thank you for being—first of all—a family of readers. And secondly, the kind of people who lift dreams up, and know when to raise a glass.

Seth: Even if we weren't family, I'd choose you every time. I'm so proud of you it makes me cry. I love you.

Julz: You have been fundamental to the success of this book in every conceivable way. Your support—emotionally and otherwise— has made my career possible. And you made my life possible! I can never fully express my gratitude. Thank you, thank you, thank you. I love you.